George, Write That Book It A Best Seller. Phillip

M000009449

THE LEGEND OF THINGS PAST

Phillip Sheppard
The Specialist
Survivor - 2016

PHILLIP WILLIAM SHEPPARD

PHILLIP WILLIAM SHEPPARD

This book is a work of fiction. Names, characters, locations, events, places, organizations and business are either the product of the authors' imagination or used fictitiously. Any resemblance to actual persons living or dead, events or locales is entirely coincidental.

Because of the dynamic nature of the Internet, any web address or links contained in this book may have change since publication and may no longer work be valid. The views expressed in this work are solely those of the author and do not necessarily reflect the views of the publisher, and the publisher herby disclaims any responsibility for them.

No part of this book may be used or reproduced by any means, graphic, electronic. Or mechanical, including photocopying, recording, taping or by any information storage retrieval system without the written permission of the publisher except in the case of brief quotations embodied in critical articles and reviews.

THE LEGEND OF THINGS PAST
Copyright © 2015 Phillip William Sheppard
All Rights Reserved

ISBN: 978-0-69242-856-6

First Edition
Published by Beyond Pluto Publishing
Cover Art Designed by The Cover Collection
Author photo by David Hume Kennerly
Printed in the United States of America

Beyond Pluto Publishing books may be ordered through booksellers or by contacting:
Beyond Pluto Publishing
930 Euclid Street, Suite 101
Santa Monica, CA 90403
310-310-0310

This book is dedicated to my mother Ernestine Winona Sheppard, my son Marcus Alexander Sheppard, my nephew Phillip Alexander, and my dog Spike

PHILLIP WILLIAM SHEPPARD

Also by Phillip William Sheppard

The Specialist: The Costa Rica Job

INSPIRATION

Steve Arrington, *Nobody Can Be You*

A Very Specials Thanks To

Kiah Danielle
Editor and Science Fiction Expert

This book would not have been possible without her extraordinary guidance in all aspects of this story. Thank you so very much.

—Phillip "The Specialist"

PHILLIP WILLIAM SHEPPARD

Table of Contents

In Memory Of

Octavia Estelle Butler
June 22, 1947–February 24, 2006

American science fiction writer.
A multiple recipient of both the Hugo and Nebula
awards, Butler was one of the best-known women in
the field. In 1995 she became the first science fiction
writer to receive the McArthur Fellowship, which is
nicknamed the "Genius Grant."

Chapter 1

"Any sufficiently advanced technology is indistinguishable from magic."

—Arthur C. Clark

May 3, 2258
Santa Monica, CA
Donovan Knight

The city's blue lights throbbed beneath the skycycle. They seemed to streak and blur as Donovan zoomed through the air, pursuing the skytrain where his target, known only as Giovanni, leapt from car to car, throwing electric grenades that exploded in yellow fingers of light. Donovan dodged the little balls of metal before they could erupt in his face. If he were hit by one of them, he would die—painfully.

Everything was quiet up there, except the beating of his heart and the wind created by his passing. The electric grenades were a completely silent technology, which made them all the more eerie.

The machine that carried him, made with the same technology as the skytrain, gave off a barely perceptible hum. He turned the speed gear to make it go faster. The train was picking up momentum as it neared the city border. Once beyond that point it would travel at three hundred miles per hour—far too fast for Donovan to keep up.

He needed to do something—quickly. The skytrain was beginning to outpace him. If he let this guy get away, the General would kill him. He might not get another mission for months. Or worse—he'd get demoted. He had worked too hard on this mission—he'd spent weeks tracking Giovanni through the city.

The criminal had been elusive. He had almost escaped. But Donovan wouldn't let him. He had yet to see the target up close, but tonight, he promised himself, he would.

The speed of Donovan's skycycle hit the maximum and Giovanni was still not within his reach. The man's black leather coat flapped madly in the torrents of air, giving the appearance that he was flying rather than jumping. Donovan was slowly falling behind.

He gritted his teeth—he knew what he needed to do.

He put his skycycle on track mode—it would follow him, using the signal on his watch.

Before he could think, before fear and logic could tell him not to, Donovan leapt from the skycycle toward the train. It took only a second but felt like minutes as he soared over the city, a thousand feet of empty space between him and the pavement below.

The train passed underneath him and for a moment he feared that he would land on one of the thin metal wires that held the cars together, or miss completely and fall to his death.

He was lucky—the impact of the cold metal pulled the breath from his lungs. Hard abs lessened the effect of the blow. He took only a moment to recover. He jumped to his feet and ran along the top of the skytrain, careful not to look over the edge. The weight of his large frame caused the metal roofs to echo with loud thumps, probably startling the passengers inside—as if the sky-chase had not already scared them out of their wits.

His target was tiring, he could tell. The wound Donovan had inflicted on Giovanni earlier was starting to take its toll. Even up here in the dark, Donovan could see the blood dripping down the other man's leg. A wound that would have left puddles on top of a groundtrain, up here sent big drops of blood splashing his way.

Donovan began to catch up. The man didn't seem to realize that he was still being followed—or maybe he had become too delirious to continue the barrage of electric grenades. Hopefully, he had run out.

Donovan was just one car behind. He could see the city limit getting closer. The skyscrapers became less frequent and the blue lights had all but faded behind them. The speed of the skytrain made it harder to move. With a great pull of energy to counteract the wind, Donovan bent his knees, tightened his muscles and pushed off.

He landed halfway onto the top of the next car. His middle crushed into the edge of it, knocking the breath from him again. The metal was slippery with a mixture of condensation and blood. Donovan almost lost his grip. He pulled himself upwards with all his might and with a last effort, rolled over onto the top.

The target was only halfway down the car. Giovanni crawled, fighting against the wind. Donovan crawled behind him, keeping his eyes only on the man's shiny black boots. Focusing on that, Donovan propelled himself forward. He reached out a hand and grabbed Giovanni by the injured leg, making him scream in pain and turn around to lash out at Donovan with his free foot. Donovan ducked and pulled the man closer. He climbed on top of him and landed a solid blow to the stomach.

The man named Giovanni doubled over, temporarily unable to breathe. He rolled onto his back, eyes wide with the shock of the blow. For the first time, Donovan was able to look at the face of his enemy head on.

He was a rather shriveled and pale person. Young, but having lived long enough for wrinkles to form under his eyes. A huge cut ran across his face from the left temple to the right side of the jaw. It was a jagged line of pink tissue, signaling just how much Giovanni had struggled when it was cut into him. Donovan had seen other members of the x5 Liberation Contingent with much cleaner initiation scars. They let the wounds heal naturally to prove they were strong enough to carry out the organization's agenda.

Seeing Giovanni's souvenir, Donovan wondered if he had been initiated by force. He didn't fit the usual profile. But, then again, how could you pick a terrorist out of a crowd? The key to x5's strength was diversity—you never really knew who would be the next attacker. Donovan would never forget the time a seven-year-old terrorist had stabbed him in the chest simply for trying to rescue her. That was x5's goal—to corrupt. To cause so much fear in the hearts of citizens that they lost faith in the authority of their government. Little kids going around knifing people and trying to blow up train stations would certainly do the trick. The terrorists wanted anarchy— then they could stage a coup—but no one knew who their leader would be.

Donovan watched the man who looked much more like a boy to him now, gasp for breath, stretching the scar where it ran across his lips. For a moment, Donovan felt pity. Maybe he could argue for a lighter sentence, considering his age. He couldn't be more than twenty-eight-years old. Then he remembered the last time he cut a criminal slack and changed his mind.

He would let the courts deal with it. It was his job to catch the criminals—nothing more. He would follow the rules, follow his orders, and everything would be fine. It wasn't up to him to decide people's fates. Besides, this boy, however naïve he may be, had plotted to kill people. He would have gone through with it had Donovan not stopped him. Surely, he didn't deserve mercy.

Donovan debated about knocking Giovanni out but decided against it. The dead weight would be too much to carry up there. Instead, he reached down and grabbed him by the shoulders of his jacket, dragging him along the car until they reached the edge. Donovan punched him in the stomach again for good measure, just to be sure he wouldn't try another escape—and maybe to vent for having had to chase him down.

Donovan hopped down on the little platform at the end of the car. The faces inside looked alarmed. The passengers were peering out the windows, looking up almost as if they could bend their line of sight to see on the roof. A few of them spotted him, a large black man in plainclothes, covered in blood, and backed away from the door. As he forced the doors open, the rest of the people caught sight of him and moved away as well. A woman screamed.

Donovan reached back to the roof and grabbed Giovanni by his oily hair. He dragged the boy down, ignoring his screams and flailing arms. Giovanni landed in a heavy pile on the floor of the platform. Donovan dragged him inside by his injured leg. His struggles had little effect on Donovan's grip. He was still trying to get air back into his collapsed lungs, which Donovan knew from experience left no energy for anything else. The boy probably thought he was dying.

Once Giovanni's lungs could pull in air again, Donovan immobilized him with electric handcuffs. He was only allowed to use them on criminals that were level seven and up— Giovanni was a level nine. The passengers stared at him. Some spoke into their palms, commanding their Liao Inserts to record the scene or dial 911. The local cops, who knew about the Army and Space Force's pursuit of Giovanni, would ignore the call and forward it to the temporary headquarters of the Army and Space Force 6th Special Forces Platoon, which Donovan commanded.

The Special Forces Platoon would ignore the call, too— they would forward it straight to him, even though they knew it would piss him off. Why forward the calls to him if they already knew he was on Giovanni's trail? He had to find these men something to do besides sit at desks answering phones, but they weren't yet qualified for much else. The General had sent him a bunch of rookies. They had their workout routines and recreational activities, but repetition could become deadening. They were sending the calls his way for fun now.

It had been a makeshift Platoon—created in Santa Monica, where Donovan lived, in answer to the threat of terrorists. The number of reports had gone up in the area, so the Santa Monica Police had called them in. The reports came mostly from insiders who wouldn't give their names—a sure sign that something huge was going on. And it was. Donovan had just caught a piece of the puzzle, which, with some interrogation, would lead him to the next piece.

Lazily, Donovan reached into his pocket. There was a scream of terror and a large, collective intake of breath. Donovan rolled his eyes and pulled his hand out, revealing a piece of gum which he popped into his mouth.

"I'm with the United States Army and Space Force," he said calmly. He held up his watch for them to see. At his command it displayed his army identification, which showed that he was a One Star General. He pointed to his captive. "This guy's a member of the x5 terrorist group. You're welcome."

With that, he dropped into the nearest empty seat, ignoring the people who got up and moved away. He rubbed his hands over his eyes, then spoke into his watch. "Connect to satellite." Sure enough, there were twenty-four missed calls from the temporary headquarters. Donovan shook his head at their idiocy. "Call General McGregor."

General McGregor was his direct superior—the one who had assigned him to this case. Donovan had notified him that he was in pursuit of Giovanni twenty minutes ago, then he'd gone dark. Though the lack of communication had its pitfalls—like no back up—if the General had constant access to bark orders into his earpiece Donovan wouldn't be able to concentrate.

"Did you get him?" The General's gruff voice came through the tiny speaker in his ear.

"Yes, sir. We're on the skytrain. The target is secure. Next stop is Los Angeles Sky Station." The watch picked up his voice even though his hand was at his side.

"Good work, General. I'll send a team there to take him to the permanent headquarters. I don't think the security at the temporary building is enough. They may try to retrieve him and it would be too easy for them. I'll send you whatever information we can get out of him. Then you can start taking down the rest of these assholes."

"Yes, sir."

"Over and out."

The line went dead. Donovan relaxed for the rest of the train ride, comforted by the knowledge that his target would not get away. The electric handcuffs sent a constant wave of small shocks through the man's body, keeping him knocked out. He would be in a lot of pain when he woke up.

Donovan stared out of the window at the blackness between Santa Monica and Los Angeles. He remembered being so fascinated in school by the idea that cities in Southern California once spread over miles and miles of land. A few hundred years ago this whole area would have been filled with light. But now cities had become like huge, tall islands, with vast swaths of wildlife in between. Many of the animals that roamed down there had once been extinct.

Donovan was surprised to see that the General had come to the station personally. He rarely went into the field these days. He was getting old. All that knowledge and experience had to stay safely tucked away at headquarters. They couldn't afford to lose him. Donovan, as highly skilled as he was, was far more replaceable.

General McGregor was an imposing man. He was a full head shorter than Donovan but still managed to make him feel like a teenager if he ever did something wrong. He reminded Donovan a little of his dad, though they looked nothing alike. For as long as he had been a part of the army, Donovan had answered to this man above all others.

No one seemed to remember a time when Hesekiel McGregor was not in charge. He was a four-star general—commander of the entire Army and Space Force, the most powerful branch of the military.

Donovan stood at attention and gave his report while General McGregor listened with an expression almost like a glare. He always looked like that—like he was on the edge of anger. But this was his neutral expression. Donovan knew him well enough to see that he was actually quite pleased.

The criminal had been loaded into a car only minutes ago, cuffs still intact around his wrists, body sagging in the arms of two privates. They dragged him in unceremoniously, knocking his head against the door twice. Donovan felt a sense of accomplishment. There had been no deaths. Tons of action, but no property destroyed.

"You did a good job," the General said. "Go home, Knight. Get some rest. You deserve it."

It was a rare moment of praise. Donovan tried not to smile. "Thank you, sir."

The General nodded and turned away. His driver opened the skycar door for him. Just before he got in, the General turned around.

"Knight?"

"Yes, sir?"

The General wore a strange expression. It was so different from anything Donovan had ever seen on that face that he couldn't place the emotion behind it.

"Take care of yourself."

"Yes, sir. Of course."

Donovan's skycycle came to fetch him only five minutes after the General and other soldiers had left the scene. It came to a gentle stop next to him, hovering six inches over the sidewalk—at the perfect height for Donovan to mount. He straddled the sleek machine, ignoring the stares of passerby. The blue lights emitting from its bottom flared almost white as he put on a burst of speed that took him into the air.

He stayed close to the ground on the way home, about ten feet up, to avoid the icy cold that came with higher altitudes. Adrenaline had kept him warm earlier, but now he would freeze up there. He connected his skycycle's system to the link rail that travelled between the two cities. It was nothing more than a fat blue strip that ran from one place to the next, about twenty feet wide. It was like a small runway that glowed in the dark—the only human technology you would ever find out here. The skycycle steered itself, following the signal of the strip, leaving Donovan's mind free to roam.

He thought about his wife, Nona, her sleeping form awaiting him in the darkness of their room. There was a pleasant anticipation at the thought of a hot shower and then sliding into bed next to her warmth. She would stir from her sleep, the silky nightgown rustling under the sheets, then turn to him, kiss his lips, and drift back off to her dream.

It always happened that way. Donovan felt comforted by that certainty, that routine. The rest of the world was never that stable, that predictable. His job was to throw himself into chaos and somehow bring order. But with Nona, the order was already there.

When he neared his high-rise apartment, he elevated his height to two hundred feet, shivering as the temperature dropped. The smooth surface of the skyscraper opened up at the click of a button on his watch revealing a large garage with two skycars—one, a 2256 Convertible Chevy Corvette, the other a 2250 SUV Lexus RX. He glided inside the garage and lowered the skycycle onto the ground between the cars. The garage door closed behind him.

He entered the house stealthily, trying not to make too much noise. The place seemed to echo twice as much now that the kids were gone. He crept into the master bedroom and was startled to see his wife wide awake, reading a book by candlelight.

Her mahogany skin shone in the glow of the small fire. Her long black hair was pulled into a messy bun. She wore a very concentrated look that he loved, as if the thing she read had completely entranced her intellect.

"Hey," he said.

She looked up at him and smiled, full lips revealing small, white teeth. "Hey. Catch the bad guys?"

Donovan smiled. "I always do. What are you doing up so late?"

"Research for the Extinct Species Revival Project."

Donovan went into the bathroom and started stripping off his bloody, sweaty clothes. It was a testament to how long they had been together that Nona didn't flinch at the sight of blood on his shirt.

"I thought you were done with that," he said through the door.

"I was, but the board decided that they need a little more information on a few of the species before we could continue."

Donovan turned on the hot water in the shower. "Don't stay up too late."

"Okay, Dad," his wife's voice sung out. "I'm almost done."

Donovan spent a long time under the water, letting the heat sink into his aching bones. By the time he was ready for bed, Nona was sound asleep, the book sitting in her lap and her head leaning awkwardly against the headboard. He smirked.

He was glad that he would be stationed in Santa Monica for a while—the city had been his home for a long time. Plus, he missed his wife when he was called away. He had used his favorable position with the General to allow him to live in his apartment instead of the temporary headquarters. He left his First Lieutenant in charge.

He shook Nona gently and urged her to lay down. She barely opened her eyes as she responded. She curled up and was asleep again within seconds. He watched her face for a moment and noticed dark circles forming under her eyes. He would have to keep an eye on her—make sure she didn't work herself to sickness.

She was so dedicated to her job she could easily stay awake for seventy-two hours straight working on some project. Once she got started, it was difficult to pull her away. He had much the same disposition. It was probably how they had managed to stay together all these years—they had started and they would finish.

Donovan stroked Nona's hair, her forehead. He kissed her cheek and joined her in bed. As much as he desired to be connected with the moist warmth of her body, he was asleep as soon as his head touched the pillow.

Chapter 2

"Time travel used to be thought of as just science fiction, but Einstein's general theory of relativity allows for the possibility that we could warp space-time so much that you could go off in a rocket and return before you set out."

—Stephen Hawking

May 4, 2258
Santa Monica, CA
Donovan Knight

Donovan always rose with the sun. Even when he wanted to sleep in, long habit forced his body into wakefulness. He left the cozy comfort of the bed without disturbing Nona and cooked breakfast.

She emerged from the room thirty minutes later, yawning and carrying a stack of papers. The night gown hugged her curvy shape.

"You're up early," he said.

"Have to work on this report. The Board wants to push it through by Friday."

Donovan looked at her for a moment. Her eyes were bloodshot. Her face seemed almost shrunken. He hadn't noticed it last night. "Well, don't work too hard. You look like you're getting sick."

"I am," Nona said. "iMed detected a virus three days ago. I took some immunity boosters, but they haven't helped much. Just have to get over it the old-fashioned way."

His wife leaned toward him across the breakfast bar. "You make any for me?" she said, nodding toward the omelet on his plate.

He smiled and pulled out more ingredients. "Of course." He slid his plate across the counter. "For you."

She smiled that cute smile of hers—the one that was a faint turning up of the corners of her mouth, showing only a few teeth. The smile was mostly in her eyes.

She ate the omelet in large bites while Donovan began making another one. Nona never pretended to be a genteel woman.

"How do you even fit all that inside you?" Donovan asked, not for the first time. It was something he always teased her about. She was average height and had arcs in her body, but she was thin.

"I have to keep up with my metabolism." She patted her stomach. "If I don't feed the monster I get in trouble."

"Yeah, so do I."

Nona was notoriously grouchy when she was hungry.

She laughed and held out her empty plate. "Another one, please."

Donovan slid the freshly made omelet to her. She dove right in. He started the process a third time, hoping he'd actually get to eat the result.

After breakfast, his wife dressed and left for her department's lab and library suite. She spent most of her time there, doing research and bringing the fossilized genes of extinct animals back to life. She would be exploring the DNA of a zebra today. It was once classified as an Equus and belonged to the Equidae family, she'd said. Donovan had seen pictures and footage of the animals. The images were so clear that it was hard to believe that they no longer existed.

Nona obsessed over bringing animals like the zebra back to earth. Donovan thought that was another reason they had stayed married—they were both driven by a desire to right the world, only Donovan wasn't sure he did as good a job as she.

Donovan went through his morning workout and shower and took his skycar to the Saint John's Providence Hospital. The twenty story building was located at the center of town, easily accessible from all parts of the city—not that it was ever much needed. The iMed App that came preinstalled on most Liao Inserts these days prevented the majority of illnesses through early detection. Donovan was a part of the dwindling group of people who refused to undergo the minor surgery for a Liao Insert. Yes, it was convenient to have information and connectivity literally at your fingertips, but Inserts were far too invasive for Donovan—even with the medical benefits. He'd rather just use a watch and make regular visits to the doctor.

Donovan entered the parking structure at the very top of the building, parked, and descended to the fifteenth floor. Inside room 1508, a permanent lodging, he found his grandfather staring blankly at the TV. A little bit of drool slid down his chin as the news anchor chattered at him.

Donovan rushed to wipe the spit from his grandfather's face with a piece of tissue from the bathroom. Even with the best care in the world, Donovan still felt that his grandfather wasn't getting enough attention.

Tobias Knight was a world-renowned scientist—the inventor of teleportation and the man who had discovered dozens of planets with his space probes. Donovan knew, unlike most people, that he had also invented a time machine—he just hadn't found a substance powerful enough to sustain it. His grandfather knew everything about everything. Physics and astronomy were his specialties, but his grandfather was well versed in biology, chemistry, and geology, too.

It somehow disturbed Donovan to see Tobias's dignity smeared by a line of drool. It was so frustrating. He knew that his grandfather would be able to solve the mystery of his illness. But, of course, if he could do that, he wouldn't be sick in the first place. His mind had slowly deteriorated with no apparent cause. He had lost his presence of mind, becoming more and more confused over time. He would wake up and not know his own name or his wife's name or Donovan's name. He wouldn't recognize his grandchildren. He would think he was in a different time—in the past, in his childhood.

Those were the worst times to be around him. When he thought he was a child again. Donovan could hardly imagine all of the horrors his grandfather had seen. Tobias had told him stories of the gruesome events of his youth but never in full detail. When his grandfather had screamed like that, it sent chills down his spine, leaving his imagination to spin out of control. What was it that he was reliving?

That had been a long time ago. Now, sitting beside this vacant, staring figure, Donovan almost wished the screaming would happen again, if only to show that there was actually someone *there*, inside the body. They had thought it was

Alzheimer's, an easily cured disease. It would have taken one shot of serum and he would have been fine.

But that wasn't it. All of the tests came back negative. Tobias Knight had a normal, healthy brain. They could only guess that his illness was completely psychological.

"Grandpa," Donovan said, holding the man's hand tightly in his own. He waited for some kind of response, knowing that he would get nothing. He could just feel the Insert that the doctors had installed in Tobias's hand—it did nothing to help his condition.

Tobias used to be a tall man with broad shoulders. Donovan had once thought that his grandfather looked a lot like an older version of himself. Today, Tobias looked like a dying version of himself—the skin under his eyes drooped down his cheeks and his soul seemed to have made an escape through the unblinking eyes.

Donovan shook the thought from his head. His grandfather wasn't dying. His body was in perfect health aside from the slow deterioration of his skin and muscles. If only Donovan could figure out what was wrong with him, what had driven him into this state of psychosis. But he wasn't the great genius that Tobias was. The world didn't know *him* as the smartest man since Steven Hawking.

"Tobias Knight," Donovan said. There wasn't even a flicker of a response in his grandfather's eyes, but he kept going, "My father was named after you. He wanted to name me after you, too—Tobias Knight the Third."

Donovan let go of his grandfather's hand and leaned back in his chair, staring at the empty face as he spoke, watching, as always, for some sign of recognition, knowing by now that it was highly unlikely. But he had to keep trying.

"I thank God to this day that my mom had the sense not to let that happen." Donovan chuckled. "Do you remember when you first started to teach me chemistry? I think I was six."

Donovan couldn't remember his age at the time, but he recalled the lessons almost perfectly. His grandfather had already become world-renowned and he wanted to share his knowledge with all of his children and grandchildren.

Tobias had given up on Donovan's father long ago. Tobias Jr. had chosen to go into the military and become a weapons expert. It was what killed him in the end. And Donovan's mother, too. She died of grief a year later. Donovan had been nine years old.

After their deaths, he went to live with Tobias for good. Donovan had lapped up his grandfather's lessons. Once, in Tobias's private lab, when he was teaching Donovan about the complicated theories of teleportation, Donovan became frustrated with what seemed impossible for his brain to absorb.

"I can't learn this," he'd said, throwing his pencil onto the counter. "It's too hard. It doesn't make any sense."

"Of course it does, boy. I learned it and so can you."

"I'm not like you. I'm not as smart." The young Donovan had stared gloomily at his notebook, refusing to look back up at the e-board. The symbols danced in his head, taunting him—never seeming to stay in the same place or to mean the same thing. One day, his grandfather would tell him how important gravity was and the next he would dismiss it altogether as a "weak" force.

"You have my genes," Tobias said, straightening his spine. Donovan could feel his grandfather's intelligent eyes drilling into him. Out of the corner of his eye, he saw Tobias turn back to the e-board. "Of course you're just as smart. You're just not trying hard enough."

"But I *am* trying." Donovan watched his grandfather hold the e-pen parallel to the e-board, about three inches away, and move it in broad strokes, erasing the equations and Greek letters.

His grandfather sighed and sat down on one of the stools in the lab. The place never seemed to be empty of stools. They were everywhere. Sleek, silver, and very uncomfortable.

"Donovan," Tobias said.

The tone of his voice forced Donovan to look at him.

"I know it's difficult," he said. It was the gentlest he had ever seen his grandfather look. "You're young. But you are smart. You *can* understand this. Just give it time."

Donovan nodded, feeling a little less glum.

"Why is it so important to you that I learn all this stuff?"

His grandfather shifted back on his stool, leaning against the wall. "Well," he said, "to me, science is..." He searched for the right words, then shrugged. "Everything."

"What do you mean?"

"'Any sufficiently advanced technology is indistinguishable from magic.' Do you know who said that?"

Donovan shook his head.

"Arthur C. Clark." His grandfather smiled. "He wasn't a scientist, but he got it just right. Science is like magic. If you push hard enough, explore deep enough, you can produce amazing things. I want to share that joy with you. The joy of giving birth to something new and beautiful."

Donovan tried his hardest at science from that point forward. He never complained again. He became the perfect student, learning in leaps and bounds. He saw the magic that his grandfather had described, but he couldn't feel it. Donovan had really enjoyed the sciences, especially physics, but they didn't invoke the same passion in him as in his grandfather.

Donovan was a mover not a thinker. Sure, he was smart—really smart—but his joy came from action, from *doing* something.

"That's why I joined the military, like my dad," Donovan said, coming back from the reminiscence. "I didn't want to disappoint you—it's just what I was made for. Like you were made for science."

Donovan stared at the immobile figure before him, wondering where all that intelligence had gone, all that passion. Tobias Knight had to be in there somewhere. He just wished there were a way for him to find out where.

Donovan rose from the hospital chair. He didn't want to go down that line of thought again. It would drive him crazy. He kissed his grandfather on the forehead and left the room.

He stopped by the nurse's station before he left, reminding them that his grandfather needed the greatest attention and care. The oldest nurse, a short, stout woman, assured him that Tobias was being given the highest quality help. She said it in that way that some doctors and nurses tended to—like you weren't intelligent enough to understand the intricacies of the medical world. "We're all very busy," her look seemed to say. "Your grandfather isn't the only patient in this hospital—isn't the only one deserving of help."

As soon as Donovan stepped into the parking garage, two uniformed men approached him. He identified them as being with the military—the Army and Space Force. He could tell by the four vertical gold stripes across the right shoulder of their navy blue uniforms. One of the men was black and bald with a round face. The other, of Hispanic descent, had short cropped, black hair.

Instantly, Donovan was worried. They never just showed up unless something extreme had happened. Was it Nona? Was it one of the kids?

"Mr. Knight," the black man said, "your presence is needed immediately at Fort Belvoir, at the command of General Hesekiel McGregor."

"What's going on?"

"That information is classified until you reach the base, sir," his partner said. "We have a skycar here to take you to the base."

"Is my family safe?"

"Sir, your family is fine. We need you to come with us."

Donovan nodded and followed them to an all-black skycar with a small American flag attached to the top. He was surprised that they would send a Magna 15—it was the fastest skycar in the army's fleet, not available to civilians. It could reach speeds of six hundred miles per hour. Civilian skycars were limited to two hundred miles per hour. Donovan's trepidation grew.

He gave a command to his watch. "Call Nona."

The bald man opened the door for him and both soldiers followed him into the back of the car. It was a lot more spacious on the inside than it looked from the outside. All three of them fit quite comfortably.

The phone rang in his ear piece. Donovan imagined Nona at home, sitting at the desk with her computer, getting down her last thought before picking up.

The skycar rose from the ground and floated out of the parking garage. The driver, whom Donovan couldn't see due to a dark partition, kept to the speed limit of ninety-five miles per hour while they were within the city. They were on a private military channel. Donovan could tell because there was no one flying at the same altitude as they were for miles around. The driver kept at a steady speed without once having to slow down for other skycars.

Finally, Nona's voice came through his earpiece, sweet and friendly but a little raspy.

Donovan explained the situation to her.

"Okay," she said, keeping the same upbeat tone.' "Be careful. Please." Donovan knew the cadences of her voice too well. She was trying to sound calm, unworried, but he could hear the stress behind the façade. She knew that this was big. Who knew what danger he was flying toward?

"I will," Donovan assured her. "I don't know how long I'll be gone yet, but I'll let you know as soon as I find out. Within..."

"Within limits." Nona finished the sentence for him. "Call me as soon as you can."

"Okay. I love you."

"Me, too."

He was about to hang up when he remembered what else he'd wanted to say. "Take some more of those immunity boosters!"

The call disconnected. He wasn't sure she had heard. He decided not to call her back—she needed to concentrate on her work. The sooner she finished, the sooner she could focus on getting better. Besides, Nona knew how to take care of herself. She had grown up in the slums of Bakersfield where advanced technology was scarce. In that city she had been exposed to all kinds of things—the least of which were bacteria and viruses.

Her family couldn't afford Liao Inserts with iMed, so they often got sick. It was a dangerous life, but it made her immune system strong.

Donovan released a long breath. Nona would be fine. He was more concerned about the fact that she was beginning to hate his job more and more. When the kids were still in the house it wasn't so bad. She was always busy with them while he was away. Now he frequently left her to an empty, lonely home.

Nona tried to hide it, but Donovan knew. She wanted him to work a desk job, but he was too young—only sixty-five. He had at least another eighty years ahead of him. He couldn't spend all that time shuffling papers. He needed air. He needed action. It put Nona in a state of almost constant worry, but Donovan knew he would be okay. He was the best at what he did. He had yet to let a target escape. Donovan had hoped that the Santa Monica terrorist case would last long enough to really patch things up. Then this.

On an impulse, he called his oldest son.

"Hey, Dad. What's going on?" Jason asked.

"I'm getting pulled from Santa Monica for an assignment. I don't know how long I'll be gone. Your mother's sick. Can you check up on her while I'm gone?"

"Yeah, I can do that. You sure everything is okay?"

Jason must have heard something in his voice. "Yeah, everything is fine."

"When are you going to get an Insert old man? You know how it looks, working for Liao and my own father won't even buy my designs?"

It was the same thing Jason said every time they talked.

"You'll get over it," Donovan said. "I already told you I'm not getting one. I can't be that accessible."

"Honestly, Dad. They're harmless."

"You talk to your brother lately?"

"Not since last week."

"Get in contact with him while I'm gone, too," Donovan said. "I need you to make sure everyone is taken care of."

"All right, Dad. Is that all?"

"That's all. I'll talk to you later."

"Okay, 'bye."

Donovan hung up the phone and breathed a sigh of relief. He couldn't leave so suddenly without knowing that someone would take care of Nona if she needed it. She would be too prideful to call one of the boys for help.

Once the skycar got beyond the city limits, the driver slowly increased speed until they were going as fast as the car could take them. Donovan tried getting more information from the two soldiers, but they wouldn't say anything more.

I apologize, sir. You'll just have to wait until we get to the base.

I'm afraid I can't tell you anything more, sir.

Always so respectful and polite but never spilling a single word of what they knew, which was probably nothing, anyway. They were only Corporals.

Donovan settled for looking out of the window at the vast forest below. There were always lush natural environments between the human cities. He thought he spotted a group of bears somewhere down there, but they were too high up for him to be sure.

When he tired of the scenery Donovan swiped his finger over the screen on his watch, occupying himself with science articles online. He expanded the screen so that the tiny projector turned on and gave him a bigger, vertical version of the site. The articles floated just above the watch, measuring about two-by -our inches.

He was just beginning to read a piece titled *Commercial Human Teleportation: The Technology Exists, so Why Doesn't the Product?* when they reached their destination. The trip had taken only fifteen minutes. They were one hundred miles outside Santa Monica. At first, they couldn't see the military airport, though the skycar's scanners could sense its presence.

The driver hovered over empty space for a moment as the security team on the ground deactivated the Mirage Builder technology. The perfect image of a patch of forest in the middle of nowhere gave way to a large clearing. The airport was utilitarian to say the least. There was one wide strip of cement to mark the runway and a couple of brick buildings for the military personnel to complete their work.

There was a jet positioned at one end of the runway, engine humming quietly. Donovan was ushered up its steps. His escorts departed then and he was left alone with the pilot. Donovan left the woman to fly the jet in peace. He didn't feel like talking. He was too busy wondering what could be going on. Thankfully, she offered him no conversation.

General McGregor had pulled him away from home for missions with little to no notice before but never without reason. He was almost tempted to call him and demand an answer, but he knew that would get him nowhere. It may even get him killed, or, at a minimum, fired. He had to be calm and rational, as his job always demanded. He took a deep breath and forcibly relaxed his muscles one by one.

Could it have something to do with the case he was already working? Was Giovanni's cell larger than they had thought? Had they unwittingly discovered a link to the nationwide underground network of x5 terrorist they'd been hunting for so long?

The thought of it filled him with excitement. It was the rush he always felt when he discovered a clue that would lead him to his target. It was like the euphoria one felt, after working on it for so long, when a puzzle or enigma is solved through a sudden stroke of genius.

Yes, maybe that was it. It would certainly warrant the immediate summons. After thinking about it for several long minutes, Donovan concluded that the terrorists had to be the answer. There was no reason for General McGregor to call him away from his current case. Donovan was the best Brigadier General in the Army, but there were plenty of other qualified soldiers of the same rank.

Donovan found himself relaxing a little. He let his mind wander over the events of the night before. He couldn't think of any details about the boy he had captured that gave any clues as to who specifically he worked with. The x5 terrorists never carried I.D.—no technology whatsoever unless it was a homemade weapon—and they never showed up in the databases either.

The Organizers—those that kidnapped children and handled the bureaucratic side of x5—raised the Attackers—those that were sent to blow up buildings and assassinate important government officials—in secret from the government. The organizers led ordinary lives on the surface, but in their basements and attics they brought up little terrors who, if they survived their missions, would grow up to be menaces to their fellow citizens.

What had Giovanni said to the interrogators to get the General so riled up? Donovan knew he'd made the right decision about him—you couldn't give criminals second chances.

But still he wondered, who was the boy's family? Had he been born into x5 or had he been snatched? Was there a couple out there somewhere still grieving for the disappearance of their child, wondering how they could have let him out of their sight, even for a moment?

Donovan knew the condition they kept the child Attackers in. He had raided enough of the places—they had rags for clothes, leftovers for meals, and drugs to make them docile or angry as needed. In less than a few years the Organizers could make a child's brainwashing absolute, but underneath the numbing confusion of drugs, their spirits were utterly tortured.

Donovan had to admit that he felt deeply sorry for those kids. He had advocated for treatment over punishment harder than anyone. The military had tried rehabilitation for terrorists under the age of thirty, but it had never worked. When he was out in the field, Donovan had to harden his heart.

Bitterly, he remembered what had come of his old acts of kindness, of sympathy. The first time was twenty years ago, when he was a Sergeant Major. He had worked x5 cases then, too. In the room temperature atmosphere of the jet's cabin, he could recall the cold night so clearly that it gave him goose bumps.

The fog had been thick in the city of Bakersfield that night.

He could barely see three yards ahead of him. It was late, but there were still people on the streets, hanging out, drinking, gambling, or selling their bodies for housing and food. From the sidewalk the cars on the street were mere shadows unless they drove past in the right hand lane. Streetlamps were almost useless.

Donovan walked the avenues of the giant slum city, pulling his hoodie tight around his cold ears. His brand new, army-issued sneakers squeaked with every step. It made him feel exposed, not only because of the noise, but because they were so uncomfortable. Would he be able to fight in these if he needed to? He couldn't believe that people spent money on these in real life.

He scanned the streets for his target, doing his best not to look too hard at any one person. He was after a young girl—an attacker. She was only a baby, really—the person who had filed the report with the army described her as nine years old. That anyone could hold this girl hostage and load her with drugs was sickening.

Donovan had convinced his superiors that he should capture her alive and take her to a psychiatric ward. They had agreed. For the first time he was eager to find his target because he wanted to help, not harm, the person. As far as the army knew, she hadn't committed any crimes yet—had not been set on innocent people like a trained dog.

The informant had given the army an address. Donovan navigated his way to it using his watch, which was strapped higher up his arm, hidden beneath the sleeves of the hoodie, and his usual tiny speakers. People around here couldn't afford skycars, let alone watches, or even the older technology of cellphones.

Though the United States outlawed groundcars in all fifty states, they had to make some exceptions for those who couldn't do better—the city of Bakersfield was littered with them. The few skycars Donovan had seen belonged to the Bakersfield Police Department. The houses, too, reflected the general squalor—they were all one or two stories, no more than five or six at maximum. These people took up a lot more space than they needed. The whole place was a boiling pot of pollution and inefficiency.

Donovan closely observed the groups that walked past him, just in case the little girl was out tonight. He could easily miss her. There were tons of kids drifting around despite the late hour.

Finally, Donovan arrived at the rundown house where the girl supposedly lived. The structure looked as if it were on its last splinter—most of the houses did. It might tumble to the ground at the slightest breath. Someone had boarded up the windows. If he hadn't been informed beforehand, Donovan would have thought that no one lived there at all.

The informant had said that she was the only child here. These Organizers were recently initiated and weren't fully trusted with the care of attackers just yet. Donovan glanced quickly around himself. No one seemed to be paying him any particular attention. He seized the moment and darted into the shadows on the side of the house. Luckily there was no gate and no dog.

He tried to find an opening in one of the windows so that he could see inside the house. The boarder had done a perfect job—he could glean nothing of the interior.

Donovan shrugged to himself.

Well, guess I'll have to go it blind.

He wished he had some kind of backup. Even an inexperienced Private would have done fine. But, along with the rest of the military, the Army and Space Force had done nothing but shrink in size since the peace treaties of 2085. War was obsolete and by extension, so was the military as it existed at that time. The U.S. Army had now adopted the Space Force—the part of the military that dealt with threats via satellite hacks and space ship attackers. Soldiers were few and far between. And they had the hardest job—finding terrorists, anarchists, and developers of biological weapons who didn't work under the authority of the government.

Donovan was often forced to work alone. It wouldn't be so bad to go in first if there were people waiting to back you from the trenches. When you were the first and last person to enter enemy territory, anything could happen. Donovan had to rely primarily on stealth. He had to get in and out quickly. Any delays could see him killed.

With a calming, deep breath, Donovan rushed the back door and kicked the area above the knob with all his might. Despite the decrepit look of the house, the door had been secured with several locks. Donovan's powerful kick sent the door sailing several feet into a big dark room.

A rustling sound came from somewhere ahead of him. From the way the sounds echoed around the walls, he guessed that there were people in a back room. He turned on the light on his e-gun, shining it rapidly into every dark space, eyes scanning his environment quickly and efficiently. The place was completely filthy. Broken dishes and torn furniture lay everywhere.

Form the back room came a hulking shape. It was a man twice Donovan's weight. Heavy flabs of stomach rolled down the front of his body. He was mostly bald, with only a few strands of hair clinging to the side of his face. His large white t-shirt was covered in greasy stains.

The man held an old fashioned .32 caliber revolver. Donovan wasn't sure who he expected to hurt with that thing. He pointed it vaguely at Donovan while he used the other hand to cover his eyes from the light. This man was an Organizer?

"Who are you?" he said in a wheezy voice that he strained to make loud. "Come any closer to my family and I'll shoot!"

"Where's the girl?" Donovan said evenly. "Give her to me."

"What girl? There ain't no girl here! Get out of my house or I'll shoot."

"I'm not going anywhere until you hand the child over. I know you have her. You stole her from a family on the west side." Donovan held his gun steady, ready to fire if he sensed danger.

An older woman's voice came from behind the man's girth. She sounded like she smoked a lot of cigarettes. Donovan could just barely see a piece of her through the doorway. "We ain't got no kids here. Please, man, don't kill us. Just leave our house. We won't even complain about the door."

Suddenly doubtful, Donovan took a step back. "Why would someone tell me that the girl was here?"

"We don't know!" the woman said, desperate. "People 'round here always stirring up some trouble. Maybe they thought you'd kill us and then they could have our stuff."

Donovan raised a skeptical eyebrow. "Got a boatload of diamonds do you?"

The man looked at the woman angrily. "Shut your mouth, girl," he whispered.

It was instinct.

Donovan acted on his most basic nature. Something just wasn't right. He rushed forward and hit the man solidly in the throat, crushing his windpipe. The gun dropped from his fingers and he slid along the wall to the floor, landing on his side. He clasped his throat as if that would reopen the airways.

The woman was quick—she dove for the gun. She raised it above her, shooting wildly toward the light of Donovan's gun.

The bullets landed in the walls and ceiling. The woman found herself out of ammunition.

Donovan kicked the gun from her hand. Instantly, she reached for another weapon, and her fingers clasped around a shard of glass.

She lunged forward. In one swift movement Donovan slid his foot forward, unbalancing her, and used her own weight to push her to the floor.

Donovan tackled her, holding the arm with the weapon away from his face. She was surprisingly strong. She screamed and kicked at him, her rancid breath blowing into his face.

"You dirty bastard! You killed my husband! You kidnapping bastard, trying to come for our little girl!"

It was the smell more than anything that almost made Donovan let go.

He held his breath and pushed his full weight onto her. He was too heavy on her chest for her to breathe. He risked releasing the weapon-free hand.

As soon as he let it go, she reached for his face.

But Donovan was a highly trained soldier. He was too fast for her. Before she even knew what was happening, he pushed two fingers firmly into the side of her neck, knocking her out cold. She wouldn't wake up for a couple of hours.

Donovan rolled over onto his back, sweat dripping over his face. He allowed himself only two seconds to recover. He jumped to his feet, waving the light of his gun back and forth over the house. He turned full circle twice before he decided that no one else was going to attack him in the main room.

He edged down the hallway, stepping over the fat man who was still struggling to breathe and keeping his back to the walls. He searched each room, the silence pressing down on his ears as he crept around.

A door creaked to his left.

He swiveled to face the sound. Down another short hallway, a door had inched open. Donovan saw a pair of eyes in the crack, round with fear.

As soon as the child realized Donovan had seen her, she pulled away from the door, leaving a black chink behind.

"It's okay," Donovan said. "I'm not here to hurt you. I want to get you out of here. Take you back to your family."

The door squeaked open a little further.

It was her. The little girl he was looking for. She matched the picture he had memorized exactly.

She wore a dirty gray dress that used to be pink. Her round face was covered in black smudges, of what substance Donovan didn't know. He could tell she had been crying recently because there were clean streaks left behind in the filth on her cheeks.

Unavoidably, Donovan's eyes fell on the ugly gash across her face. It zigzagged back and forth on its way down from her left temple to the right side of her jaw.

This child had fought. Had screamed.

Donovan felt a crushing pain in his chest. He forced away the image of a cluster of hands holding her to a table, all of them eager to see her bleed for x5.

"Please." He lowered his gun and reached out a hand to her. "Come with me. I'll take you to a safe place. And then we can find your family."

"You can take me to Momma?"

"Yes, honey. Come with me."

Tentatively, the little girl came out. Donovan saw that the door led down into a basement.

"Was there anyone else down there with you?"

She shook her head.

Donovan was relieved. He had no desire to see the horrors that lay down there.

"What's your name?" he asked.

"Mae." Her voice came out softly.

"That's a pretty name, Mae. Are you ready to leave this place?"

She nodded.

"Good." Donovan smiled and held out his hand.

Mae didn't smile back, but she put her hand in his. There was something sticky and black on her palms, but Donovan ignored it and clasped her hand firmly.

He ducked into the backyard, aiming his gun in one hand and pulling the girl behind him. They crouched behind a small tree. When Donovan saw no sign of attackers, he crossed into the yard of the neighbors behind and walked along the side of the house, trying to look as if he belonged there.

Before they emerged onto the street, he bent down next to Mae.

"I'm going to have to carry you now." Donovan took off his hoodie and pulled it over her head. It fell to her knees and she almost disappeared under the hood. "We don't want anyone to see you and try to take you back, right?"

Mae nodded. Donovan scooped her up. In his muscled arms she weighed no more than a pillow. He carried his load onto the street and headed in the direction of his skycycle which he had hidden in a copse of trees in a remote part of the city.

It wasn't long before people started to stare. He kept walking, eying them cautiously. Why were they looking at him like that?

Donovan heard rapid footsteps behind him. Someone was following.

He picked up his pace.

As he turned a corner near a grocery store, a woman leaning against its wall called out to him.

"Nice watch you got there."

Donovan's heart almost stopped. He cursed himself. How could he forget to take off his watch?! A stupid, rookie mistake. He ignored the woman and kept walking. But she had called the attention of others nearby. Even more people looked his way.

Donovan walked a little faster and listened carefully to the pursuers on the sidewalk behind him. One... two... three people. Two were average weight and the other was really small. He could tell by the different sounds their shoes made when they hit the ground.

"Can I see that watch, Pops?" a young boy said as he rode his bike in the gutter alongside Donovan.

"Where you from?" an older man leaning on a lamppost asked him. "You not from around here." Luckily, the man didn't feel like pursuing the matter. When Donovan did not slow or acknowledge him, the man spit on the ground. "Don't come back here again."

The boy on the bike still trailed him. "You don't belong here, *pris*. Get out of here before you get hurt. Leave that little girl here. She's one of us."

Should he just run for it? Or should he put the girl down and fight. He ruled against the latter option. How long before other people started to jump in? He could probably take down fifty men on his own but only five of them at a time. If he turned and fought right now, even with the element of surprise, Mae might get caught in the scuffle. He might lose track of her. If he ran, he could probably make it. He was fast, and he could already hear one of them breathing heavily behind him.

He had to do something.

Donovan made his decision in an instant and slipped into action. He shifted Mae in his arms. "Mae, no matter what happens next, I need you to hang onto me and not let go. Can you do that?"

"Yes."

"Okay, you have a good grip?"

He felt her hair brush his face as she nodded. Felt the sticky substance from her hands touch his neck.

"On the count of three, I'm going to run. Hold on tight."

Donovan looked around. More people had emptied into the streets—news of his presence had spread like a deadly virus.

"One...two..."

Before a crowd could form around him and block him in, Donovan broke into a run.

"Three!"

A long moment passed before anyone reacted. It was the perfect amount of time for Donovan to disappear around another corner into a less populated alleyway.

There were three more turns before he reached his skycycle. The distance was about five blocks. He heard people behind him shouting, "He went that way! Over there!" The followers had figured out where he had gone and now others in the neighborhood had joined them.

Who were all these people who wanted it out for him so badly? Were they after Mae? They couldn't possibly *all* know her.

Donovan shook the puzzle out of mind and focused on speed. Luckily, some of the heavier ones couldn't keep up with the cardio and quickly fell behind. He could run at his current speed for fifty miles. None of them were able to keep up. He doubted any of them ever exercised, and the neighborhoods here were flooded with processed foods. It was the only stuff they could afford.

Donovan turned sharply around another two corners. Mae almost slipped from around his torso. He could feel her hands beginning to sweat against his neck. Suddenly, the group of people decided to give up chasing him. He slowed his pace but kept running.

"Don't worry, Mae. We're going to be all right. We'll make it out of here."

He had relaxed too soon.

A heavy body crashed into him from the left, throwing both him and Mae to the ground. His head banged against the cement, blurring his vision. He found his way to a standing position. He looked around for Mae and was surprised to see her leaning causally against the wall. She looked him directly in the eyes and smiled.

It wasn't the grin of a child—there was no joy in her eyes. She flashed him the smile of a coy adult. He frowned at her. "Mae?"

The man who had delivered the amateur tackle was slowly getting to his feet, drawing Donovan's attention. He whipped his e-gun out of the holster and pointed it at him. The man did not seem disturbed by the weapon—he just looked into the alleyway from which he had emerged.

"There he is, boss," he said. "Donovan Knight."

How does he know my name?

Who was Donovan Knight to the slums of Bakersfield? Why did he matter to them? Donovan turned the e-gun toward the alley and spotted a man as much out of place as he was. He was short but beefy, dressed in a black suit with a purple tie. He had a prickly mass of short grey hair on his head. His black shoes shined against the dirty pavement.

Donovan backed up several steps so he could have both men in his range. He glanced over his shoulder to make sure no one else was there.

The suited man flashed him a toothy grin. "You should be honored, Donovan. You've been selected to serve as my example to the Army and Space Force what I think of them. It was me who sent the man who reported Mae's location." He chuckled heartily. "I'm going to kill you."

Donovan held his gun steadily on the suited man. He was the more nonchalant of the two—very relaxed and poised, but there was a catlike way to his mannerisms. The man was in a state of false tranquility—he appeared completely at ease, but he was ready to spring at any moment.

This man was an expert fighter, Donovan knew just by looking at him. No wonder the tackler stood back. His boss didn't need his protection. He had just needed his servant to get dirty for him. No man in a suit that nice was going to tackle another man to the ground.

"Who are you?" Donovan asked.

"Why," the man looked astounded, "I'm the leader of x5, of course. My name is Petridge."

Donovan was stunned.

"Yes, yes, everyone always has that reaction. The Organizers' initiation markers are a little more subtle." The man pulled up his sleeve to reveal a long, ropey scar that stretched from his wrist all the way to his armpit. He shook the sleeve down.

"As I was saying," Petridge said lazily, "I lured you here to kill you..."

Donovan wasn't listening anymore. This man had confessed to being a member x5. That was all the permission he needed to shoot him. Donovan discreetly shifted the gear on his e-gun to fatal.

The man shook his finger. "Ah, ah, ah. You wouldn't want to do that." He walked over to Mae and put his arm around her shoulder. In a movement so fast Donovan barely saw it happen, the man snatched Mae into his grasp and put his thick arm around her neck.

With his free arm, he pulled out a silver shaving knife. Donovan had never seen one in person before—only in old movies. The man held it firmly to Mae's neck. The little girl's eyes opened wide in terror. She let out of a quiet, crying moan.

"Let her go," Donovan said.

"Why should I do that?" The man pushed the knife just so, and beads of blood dripped down Mae's neck. Anger flashed through Donovan's body.

He was completely unaware of what happened next until it was already over. He took a step forward and pulled the trigger of his e-gun. The small ball of blue light struck Petridge directly in the forehead, avoiding Mae by mere inches.

The man collapsed to the ground, twitching as if he were having a seizure. His body would not still for several minutes, but he was already dead. Donovan turned to the other man who put up his hands and backed away.

"Please don't kill me."

Too exhausted mentally to deal with him, Donovan turned to Mae, who stood stiffly against the wall. She was breathing hard and her arms were shaking.

"Mae," Donovan said. "Let's get away from here." He wanted to leave Bakersfield as quickly as possible. His skycycle was only another half-mile away.

"Mae!" The tackler had not left the scene as Donovan had assumed. "Come with me. You belong to us. Don't go nowhere with that *pris*."

Mae looked at him as if in a daze. Donovan moved slowly toward her.

"Mae!" the man shouted. "He killed your father right in front of you. Remember your *oath*!"

The tackler's final word seemed to trigger a dormant rage in Mae. Her eyes burned with anger and hatred.

"It's okay, Mae," Donovan said gently. "I didn't kill your father. I won't hurt you. No one will ever hurt you if you just come with me."

"Come with *me*, Mae. We're your real family out here." The man came closer.

Mae looked at him with narrowed eyes, as if suspicious of him.

"That man is not your family," Donovan retorted. "His boss almost killed you."

The fire in her eyes seemed to dim and her breathing calmed. Donovan reached out his hand. Mae grabbed it as if transfixed.

In half a second, the little girl's face transformed into a twisted mask of emotion. Donovan hadn't expected it, hadn't prepared for something like this. She was only seven years old—how could she possibly...?

In the instant that her face had changed, Mae slipped her hand into the pocket of her dress and drew a short, sharp blade. It was rusty from long disuse. Donovan wanted to tell her to put to it away, that she didn't know what it was like to kill a man, that it would be a stain on her soul forever. He couldn't get the words out of his mouth quickly enough—the girl leap forward and struck with all her strength.

Never had it occurred to Donovan that she would use the knife on him.

The metal penetrated perfectly between his ribs, digging into his lung. He stared at the small child as the pain ripped through him. That couldn't have been just luck. She had been trained—trained to go for the vitals. She knew exactly what she was doing.

But why him? Why did she stab him?

Donovan would never forget that face, the twisted scar cutting across the gleeful smile that played on her lips. He sagged to his knees then dropped to the ground like a sack. He had been stabbed once before, but it had felt nothing like this.

There was something wrong. His heart was shuddering.

It was going to explode. His panic only made the spasms come faster.

As Donovan lay helpless, Mae (was that even her real name?) searched his pockets. She found the roll of paper money and the plastic credit cards that the General had issued him for this mission—no one here used electronic funds.

Mae kicked him in the side and spit on the ground next to him.

She bent over his face. "There was a paralysis potion on that knife. I'm going to do what my father planned for you."

The next few minutes were the longest and most gruesome of Donovan's life. The little girl, like a demon of hell, calmly drew her blade across his face, slicing through the flesh like butter, pushing it down until it touched bone.

It was then that Donovan realized that Mae believed the man he shot to be her father. How had he gotten her to believe that? Even after he cut her neck?

Donovan's nerve endings screamed, blotting out all thought. They screeched so loudly in his ears that the sound became like a big wave that enveloped him, drowned him. His mind was on fire—he wanted to shout, to shriek out the throbbing, piercing hurts, but the paralysis allowed him only to lie there, staring. When the initiation rite was complete, Mae stood up and looked down on him. It was the oddest image—the moon shone behind her head, giving her a halo, but her face, permanently scarred and plastered with a smile that stemmed from causing pain, was anything but angelic.

"Don't come back here, *pris*," he heard her say. His vision had started to fade. "You will never be one of us and I will never be one you."

She stuffed the crumpled bills into her pocket and ran off, leaving Donovan to choke on his own blood.

Chapter 3

"Life on earth is at the ever-increasing risk of being wiped out by disaster, such as sudden global nuclear war, a genetically engineered virus or other dangers we have not yet thought of."

—Stephen Hawking

May 4, 2258
En Route to Fort Belvoir, VA
Donovan Knight

The sudden turbulence jerked Donovan out of his memories—memories that he still couldn't quite believe. The world was full of evil things and he had finally switched out his worn and battered naiveté in favor of objectivity. Objectivity was what kept him alive, brought him back to his wife and kids.

Some holy soul in Bakersfield had called the police that night. They did it anonymously, so Donovan never got to thank them.

He heard the sirens as soon as Mae's feet disappeared around a corner. They would probably never find her. The immediate hospital attention had saved Donovan's face. It took weeks to heal, but when it did, there wasn't even a scar left behind.

The damage was on the inside. Something about being betrayed by such a young soul, a person who should have been innocent and pure, disturbed him far beyond any scar she may have left behind. Sometimes he dreamed about it. He would feel her blade all over again, cutting into his flesh as if he were nothing more than a slice of fish. He would wake up soaked in sweat, his heart thundering. Donovan had learned that day that, for the sake of his own life, he could never show mercy again.

The world was screwed—he just had to do his best to unscrew it without getting killed first.

When the pilot landed the plane just outside Fort Belvoir, Donovan glanced at the time to see that only two and a half hours had passed.

To the naked eye there appeared to be nothing there but an empty field and a stone archway. The security there was far stricter than at the airport. They couldn't get in without first confirming their identities.

The pilot turned off the jet's engines.

"Shall we?" she said, gesturing to the door.

"Yes. I'm Donovan Knight by the way. Sorry I didn't introduce myself, I was a little... preoccupied."

The woman gave a small smile. "No problem. I hear this is supposed to be really important. Top secret and all that." She reached out a hand to him. "Christina Austin."

Donovan shook the proffered hand.

They walked up to the stone archway together, boots stirring up little clouds of dust.

"Brigadier General Donovan Knight reporting."

"Corporal Christina Austin reporting."

The image in front of them blurred, and an electronic voice came from seemingly nowhere.

"Please step forward." It was the voice of the military identification system—Idem.

They got closer to the archway.

"Please look straight ahead without blinking and hold up your hands, palms facing outwards."

They followed the instructions. A bright light shone into their eyes and something warm passed over their hands. Despite the warning, Donovan always blinked. It took only two minutes for Idem to match their fingerprints, irises, and blood samples to the ones on record.

"Your identity has been confirmed." Idem released the Mirage Builder and the fort came into view. It was like watching a TV turn on—one moment there was nothing, the next, a complete image. They walked through the temporary portal. As soon as they stepped through the stone archway the fort became invisible to outsiders again.

Fort Belvoir was the oldest military base in the United States. While many of the others fell into decline over the years as war became scarce, the government kept Fort Belvoir in working order. The nations of the world were at peace, but there were still plenty of criminals to deal with—drug dealers, thieves, murderers. But those kinds of people were below Donovan's paygrade. It was his job to catch the people who threatened national or world peace.

Fort Belvoir was on a huge plot of land, most of it used to grow food and raise animals. There were two massive buildings, sleek with glass tinted black. A thin, elegant bridge connected them. One was about nine stories taller than the other. Donovan knew from previous visits that those extra nine stories were off limits to everyone except those chosen by the General to have access. A white access card would be linked to their Idem profile. When they no longer needed access, the card deactivated.

As far as Donovan knew, no one had used those extra floors in years. Didn't have an emergency big enough, he guessed.

Christina led him to the taller building. The glass doors slid apart to allow them entrance then closed behind them with a soft *whoosh*. There was a sense of finality about it. Donovan was surprised to see that the place was busy with soldiers. They rushed across the room in both directions, in small groups or individually, their shiny shoes clacking against the tiles. They whispered to each other urgently and glanced in his direction as they passed. Many of them recognized him, expected him even, judging by the unsurprised looks on their faces.

Five people manned the information desk in the center of the floor. All but one of them was busy with phone calls. The free man's eyebrows shot up at the sight of Donovan.

"Brigadier General Knight, sir," he said, emerging from behind the counter and almost tripping as he stubbed his toe on the corner. "Ouch—we've been expecting you. I'm Private Cole. I am to escort you to the General. Please, follow me."

"I'm afraid this is where I leave you," Christina said.

Donovan said goodbye and followed Private Cole to the elevators. The Private raised his palm to a sensor on the right, and a red light, in the shape of credit card, shone from his hand. It was a minimal security pass—it allowed him to get into things like store rooms, file cabinets, and, of course, elevators.

Donovan watched the numbers light up as they ascended. It was a quiet ride. They stopped at floor fifty-one. The door opened to reveal another elevator directly across the hall.

Private Cole turned to face him.

"I have your access card here, if you'd like to sync Inserts."

"Don't have one," Donovan said. "But I think my watch will suffice."

Donovan held his wrist next to the Private's palm.

"Transfer Brigadier General Knight's access card," Private Cole said.

Instantly, Donovan's watch beeped and a white card hovered above its surface. Then it disappeared. Donovan's inventory now held a white access card. He was astounded. His stomach clenched with both worry and excited anticipation. They must have found the national leader of x5 cells. That had to be it. Right? No, maybe they had discovered that x5 was worldwide.

It had to be the world, not just the country, to warrant a white access card. The way the staff scurried to and fro down below almost nervously, as if hysteria were just about to break open, affirmed his suspicion.

"Thank you, Private." Donovan dismissed the clumsy solider.

"General McGregor is expecting you on floor fifty-five, sir."

Donovan nodded and the Private vanished behind the elevator doors. After holding his watch to the sensor on the left of the elevator, Donovan stepped inside and pressed number fifty-five. Silence engulfed him. Again, he felt that sensation of nervousness. He wanted to know what was going on so he could jump into the action. He needed to *do* something.

The doors opened to pandemonium. For the first three seconds, Donovan was only aware of papers and manila folders soaring in the air like birds. Rows upon rows of desks lined the huge room which spanned the entire fifty-fifth floor. There were soldiers everywhere, of every rank, all of them tripping over each other in their haste to reach their destinations. The ones who were sitting were no less calm—they typed frantically at their computers, eyes never leaving the screens. Many of them rubbed their temples or pulled at their hair. Voices rose and fell in loud clamors.

He grabbed the nearest person by the arm—a little roughly in an effort to snap her out of the frenzy that had taken over the room. The woman's blonde ponytail whipped around as Donovan pulled her to him. She stared at him, eyes unfocused, mouth gaping like a fish.

"Where's General McGregor?"

She looked toward the back of the room. Donovan followed her gaze and spotted the General standing behind a desk on a raised platform, barking out orders at everyone around him. Donovan headed over, dodging soldiers as he went.

The General spotted him as he approached.

"Brigadier General Knight!" he called in a booming voice.

Donovan shook the General's hand.

"Just the man we need." General McGregor didn't smile. He almost never did. But his shoulders relaxed infinitesimally and the creases on his forehead lessened—the closest to relieved anyone would ever see him.

The General held up his hand to silence the crowd around him.

"Everyone take fifteen. Reassemble here at 1705 hours." The soldiers dispersed. A few of them looked disappointed.

"Follow me, Knight." The General turned away without waiting for a response. Donovan followed him to a silver door tucked away in a corner of the room. The General swiped his palm across the access pad. A black card appeared and disappeared—the right of admittance to any and everything at any time. He was the second most powerful man in the nation—right after the president. The other military branches were practically extinct. The leaders of them were really only in honorary positions.

The General gestured for Donovan to enter first. Once the door was secured, he sat behind a large desk with a glass surface. The computer installed inside it projected an image of the General's family on vacation somewhere tropical, all smiling like they were having the time of their lives. Then it switched to a picture of the General shaking hands with the President. The images continued to shift as the leather seat creaked under the General's weight. Donovan sat across from him and waited. It was never a good thing to pester General McGregor with a lot of questions. Best to let him do all the talking first.

"As you could see out there, we're in a bit of a panic."

Donovan thought that "a bit" was an understatement but kept the thought to himself. The General looked Donovan directly in the eyes. He had a stern stare—not unkind but clearly unwilling to tolerate any defiance.

"I have a mission for you."

Well, that was obvious.

"It involves exposing you to top secret information. And I mean information you cannot share with anyone—not your wife, not anyone."

"I understand, sir."

The General held up a hand.

"This mission, if you accept it, will possibly cost you your life."

Donovan couldn't resist. "I always risk my life, sir."

"That's not what I meant. The nature of this assignment involves—things—that may change your life as you know it. What you choose to do may change the world as we know it."

Donovan shifted in his seat. "Sir, can you just tell me what's going on?"

The General sighed. This, more than anything he had seen so far, increased Donovan's trepidation. A tingle of fear began to leech into the pit of his belly.

"Donovan."

Donovan frowned. The General *never* used his first name, even at informal events.

"This mission demands that you sacrifice everything."

Donovan stared at him. There was something wrong here. "Sir..."

"Are you willing to accept that?"

"...Yes."

The General nodded. "Good." He cleared his throat. "If you accept, I will give you the access card you need so I can release classified information."

In answer, Donovan held up his wrist. The General transferred an access card to Donovan's watch. It was black.

"Sir, what's going on? Why do I need a black card?"

The General stood up and began to pace. Once again, Donovan's mind was blown. The General was such a steady, calm man. Donovan had always admired him for it—he was always in perfect control of his emotions.

The General's nervous energy transferred over. Donovan began to tap his foot rapidly on the floor.

"Understand, even with a black card, I can't tell you everything. You can't know the full details of the mission until you reach your destination."

Before Donovan could ask where he would be going, the General rushed on.

"But here's what you can know: there has been a massive biological attack on the world. It started here in the U.S. and has since spread to every country on the planet. Millions of people have been infected with a deadly virus—it attaches to the genes, becomes indistinguishable from them, and appears benign for several years, then it suddenly starts to attack the host. We're not sure what triggers it, but people are slowly dying everywhere. Most of them don't even know it yet. It's slow-acting."

A suspicion began to form in Donovan's mind. "This virus..."

The General nodded as if knowing what Donovan was thinking. "Yes. It's the same benign virus that was found in your blood all those years ago. You were the first known case. And now it's everywhere. Everyone at this base has it. You have it. I have it. I have confirmed that your wife and children have it, as well. You're wife's condition is the most advanced of your family."

Donovan's heart seemed to stop. His brain froze. That's why the General was acting so strange. He was dying. They all were. Maybe even the General's own family.

This was the reason his wife had looked so ill recently. It wasn't that she was being overworked; it was this virus—a virus that likely started with him. Flames of hot anger licked through his insides. His sight was smeared with the force of it. Whoever had done this would suffer for it.

Donovan's face was hot. "Why didn't you tell me? Are you saying that I caused this?"

"We're not accusing you of anything. And, again, I can't tell you the details of what I know. Not yet."

Donovan had to shake his head to clear away the fury. If he didn't calm himself and think rationally, he didn't know what stupid things he might say or do.

"How long?"

The General looked grim. "We don't know. We hope we can avoid this disaster altogether."

"Are you looking for a cure? Sir, I don't see how I can help with this. I should be going after the people responsible."

"You will. The cure is plan B. What we'll be doing is sending you back in time."

"What?" Donovan was angry again in an instant. There was no time for games. He didn't understand what the General meant and didn't have the patience to listen to an explanation. He fought with the rage, tamping it down.

"Your grandfather successfully built a time machine back in 2170."

"*2170?* But I worked with him on it. He didn't have a power source—"

"It's likely that Tobias was testing you. To see if you could figure out a solution on your own, like he had."

Donovan was stunned. Time travel had been available this whole time and his grandfather never shared it with him.

"When Tobias shared his invention with my predecessor, he requested that Tobias not reveal it to anyone—that it remain a government secret only to be used in the worst of times."

"And as an employee of the government, of course, he had to obey."

"Yes—but it wasn't by force. Tobias, I think, understood the implications and possible consequences of time travel more than anyone. Only a very few people know the technology exists—Tobias, the President of the United States, the heads of all four branches of the military from 2170 onward—and now you."

There was a long pause. There wasn't enough time to assess all this—not enough time for him to wrap his mind around the idea of time travel. What would happen if he went back in time and changed something that wasn't meant to be changed? Could he stop himself from ever existing? Could he stop himself from ever having met his wife? Having children? Not just any children but *his* children?

Now he understood what the General meant. It wasn't about sacrificing his life—it was about sacrificing his identity, his family, which was far worse. But if he didn't do this, then...

"Donovan," the General said, "the world needs you now more than ever. We have an idea of who's behind this..."

"Who?"

The General tilted his head. There was an odd expression on his face. Donovan was almost getting used to this new

General—the one who had facial expressions, who felt things, who paced the floor with such energy. He thought that he might like him even.

"I can't tell you that." General McGregor looked—what? Sad? Frustrated? "All of the details of this mission are classified until you actually go back."

"Go back to when?"

"I can't tell you that either."

Donovan restrained the urge to kick the desk. He drew in a deep breath and let it out slowly.

"Okay," he said, "When do I go?"

"Now." The General tapped something on his palm and there was a dim whirring sound to the right. The scenic picture of a boat on a lake surrounded by mountains disappeared—there had never been a picture there to begin with. It was just a projection.

Hidden behind the illusion was a small tubular room made of metal. Donovan recognized the design from his grandfather's prototypes. The only difference was that this one glowed with a blue light—it worked.

The General motioned for him to step inside. Donovan became very nervous. He wasn't used to this—the unknown. He had always been able to see his enemies clearly. He wasn't sure if he wanted to do it. He hesitated in front of the machine.

"I need to call my wife. Let her know that I'll be gone..."

The look on General McGregor's face gave him the answer. "You can't call her. Besides, if you fix things in the past, you'll never be sent on this mission."

"But..."

"Brigadier General Knight..." Donovan was a little startled at the General's return to formality. The man's face was perfectly neutral now. He wondered where that other General had gone—and if he would ever see him again. "May I remind you that the entire human race is relying on you? Including your wife and children."

Donovan straightened his shoulders and stepped inside the machine. He looked at the General through the glass door. The General stared gravely back.

"I'm transferring the brief to your watch. Do not open it until you arrive at your destination."

"Yes, sir." Suddenly his watch seemed to burn at his side, a secret nugget of information calling his name. "I don't suppose you can tell me where I'm going at least?"

The General's lips twitched. Maybe that other guy was still in there somewhere. "Nowhere... They'll be expecting you."

Before he could ponder this, the General tapped his palm and Donovan was sucked into a whirlpool of white and blue light.

Chapter 4

"The truth is, we're all cyborgs with cell phones and online identities."

—Geoff Johns

May 4, 2176
Fort Belvoir, VA
Donovan Knight

Donovan felt as if he were being sucked down a drain. He was being pulled so hard and so fast that he couldn't move his body. He could do nothing but sink into the terror of temporary paralysis. Any effort to shift even an inch resulted in a strain in his muscles that left him weak.

He could do nothing but ride it out. His head was spinning, then splitting. He felt pain beyond anything he had ever felt before—worse than being shot with a fatal setting on an electron gun, worse than third degree burns from explosions, worse than having his face cut open by a nine-year-old. He didn't know what to do with the agony—he blacked out.

When Donovan came to, the motion of the time machine had slowed. His brain seemed to expand under his skull, to pulsate as if to the ticking of a clock. Tick-throb, tock-throb. Exhausted from the pain that had ripped through him, he drifted back into unconsciousness.

When he woke the second time, he stayed awake. The time machine had come almost to a stop. The feeling now resembled a descending elevator that slowly rotated. The white and blue blur that surrounded him began to fade in places, revealing human faces. But the spinning kept any of them from becoming clear.

Finally, the machine stopped and the whirlwind of light died.

At first, Donovan thought that the time machine hadn't worked and was angry and sick at the thought that he would have to endure another trip like that. Then he realized that the office outside the time machine was similar to the one he had left but not exactly the same. There was a desk in the same place, but it was different desk. The same plant in the far corner, but it was much shorter. And the man leaning against the desk looking at him was not General McGregor.

The doors to the time machine opened and Donovan reluctantly exited.

He stood before a man of medium height. A Caucasian man, balding slightly, dressed in a General's uniform. He had a thick, bristly, white mustache to match his hair. This man held the same position as General McGregor in the present— or future? He supposed technically this *was* the present.

"Brigadier General Knight," the man said. After dealing so long with the booming voice of General McGregor, this man's voice seemed absurdly weak.

Donovan fought the urge to laugh at him.

"I've been expecting you. Please sit down," the past— present—General said as he took his own seat behind the desk.

Donovan sat, having an intense sensation of déjà vu.

"I am General Cornelius Umar, predecessor to General Hesekiel McGregor. It is my understanding that you will be briefing me—and a small team that I will personally select—about this case. I received a message from General McGregor, but I'm afraid he didn't give me very many details. All I know is that there is a biological threat that needs to be prevented."

"I'll be briefing the both of us, sir," Donovan replied. "I don't know much, myself. I was sent here on the condition that I know nothing about the mission until I arrived. Speaking of which, what year is this?"

"2180." General Umar said.

"Eighty-two years." Donovan could not comprehend that he had actually travelled back that amount of time.

"Yes. Quite a long time ago, eh?"

"Yes, sir."

"Shall we get started?" General Umar looked expectant.

"Oh—yes—the information is here on my watch, sir."

"Your watch?" General Umar said. "They still have watches eighty-two years from now? I would have thought they'd come up with something new by then."

"They have," Donovan said. "They're called Liao Inserts—a watch inside your body, basically. It requires a minor surgery—they insert tiny pieces into your hands and ear. The screen appears on your palm—or palms, if you hold them together to get a bigger screen.

"Inserts are connected to everything, but so is my watch—it's my phone, the key to my car and my house, my credit card, my full time nurse, and my black clearance card that enabled me to be sent back in time."

Those last words felt absurd coming out of his mouth. *Sent back in time.*

"We still use watches for all that, too—except the nurse thing. We don't have that kind of technology yet. What does it do, monitor your heartbeat?"

"Yes, and my blood. It can do that without breaking the skin. So it catches illnesses before they fully develop. With technology like that, I don't think Inserts are all that necessary for me."

General Umar's eyes were round like a child's. "Fascinating. I would love to learn more about 2258, but I'm afraid this isn't the appropriate time. We have more important matters to attend to. Can you send the brief to me?"

"Sure." Donovan scanned through the screen on his watch until he found the brief in his inventory. He pulled up his email and typed in the address that General Umar gave him. He hit send and waited for the high-pitched *ping* that meant it had gone through. Instead, the watch beeped rapidly three times. A notice appeared:

ACTION RESTRICTED

General Umar nodded. "I guess General McGregor doesn't want that stuck in the past for someone to find. Fair enough. You have text reader on that watch I presume?"

"Yes, sir."

"Let's hear it. Then I will decide who would be best to assign to this case."

Donovan selected the file and expanded it until a 3D version floated in front of him. He would read along with the audio.

He hit the play button. General McGregor's voice came through clearly, as if he were standing right next to them.

Good evening, General Umar, Brigadier General Knight. I'm General Hesekiel McGregor, four-star general in command of the United States Army and Space Force in the year 2258.

This is a highly classified information brief. No one outside the addressees may know the contents of this file except by the disclosure of General Umar. No copies shall be made of this brief for any reason. The purpose of this briefing is to bring you up to date on the investigation of the biological attacks on the United States, which spread to the entirety of the human race between the years 2223 and 2258.

The years 2223 to 2258 marked the exact time that Donovan had spent in the army.

This investigation has its roots in the discovery of a benign virus that attached itself to the genes of one Private Donovan Knight.

General Umar gave him an accusing look. Donovan didn't meet his eye. If General Umar didn't like that, then he certainly wouldn't like what was coming next. It seemed General Umar was willing to wait patiently until the recording finished—he didn't make a sound, though his face became stonier as each word spilled out of Donovan's watch.

We kept an eye on Donovan from that day forward. For many years it seemed that the virus would remain harmless. However, in 2228, we began to find affected genes in other soldiers. We called for an immediate quarantine, but the virus continued to spread in spite of our efforts.

Donovan remembered that. He had been infuriated when the army soldiers burst into his home, frightening his children with their alien-like masks. They lined the walls with a biologically impenetrable plastic and sealed them off. They were stuck there for weeks. The army provided cheap groceries when their food ran out. They ate beans and vegetables out of cans for a month before they were allowed to leave the apartment again.

There were reports that doctors were discovering it in the genes of civilians as well. In a matter of weeks, thousands of people were infected. It was clear that the quarantine was pointless so we terminated it.

Top government officials, including myself, consulted on the issue and we decided that there would be an ongoing investigation into the source of the virus. The first known case was Private Donovan Knight, who had since been promoted to Staff Sergeant. We kept a very close eye on his movements and on his blood, but there was nothing suspicious about him or any of his acquaintances. We'd thought that an enemy of Donovan's had possibly done this to him—maybe the person was hiding in plain sight, pretending to be his friend. But we found nothing. The virus remained dormant.

Donovan was a little disturbed that General McGregor had had him spied on for so many years, that he hadn't told Donovan that the virus had spread. Didn't the General trust him?

Staff Sergeant Knight was cleared as the source of the virus when I received a message in the time machine in 2233. It read: "It's not Donovan. Investigate Tobias Knight." It was signed "Code T.M.A.C.P.U.—May 31, 2258"

Donovan paused the feed. He stared at General Umar, who gave him a quizzical look.

"Tobias Knight? Are you two...?"

Donovan didn't want to say it out loud, didn't want to believe what he'd just heard, but the words came out of his mouth as if of their own accord. "He's my grandfather."

The General frowned. "Your grandfather? If that's true then why did General McGregor assign you to this case? You're too close."

Donovan just shook his head. *What the hell was going on here?* "I don't know. Like I told you, I didn't know what the mission was about until now. I don't know what General McGregor was thinking. Maybe there's an answer somewhere in the brief. There has to be an explanation."

"Are you all right?" General Umar said. "You look like you're going to be sick."

Donovan was. He felt his stomach churning with nausea. He didn't feel like himself. He wasn't usually this reactive. He took a deep breath and gathered his emotions under control. "I'm fine."

General Umar looked skeptical.

"I'm okay. I just—that was unexpected."

"I daresay."

"It can't be true. My grandfather would never do this."

Where was the proof? If they were going to accuse his grandfather, they had to at least present evidence.

"We can continue when you feel ready. But if it gives you any comfort, your grandfather will be okay for now—he's innocent until proven guilty. He would still have to go to trial."

"It's not his safety I'm worried about, it's his name." His grandfather was no longer in a position to defend himself.

The General raised his eyebrows. "The best way to defend his name is to get to the bottom of this virus. I know Tobias personally—I never would have guessed he'd do something like this. But they wouldn't send a message to the past for nothing. We have to complete the mission. Then we'll know what's what."

Donovan, seeing no way around it, pressed the play button, trying his best to listen objectively. He had to come up with his grandfather's defense. Whatever evidence they had— it was wrong. He would find some way to dispute it.

As General Umar already knows, the acronym stands for Time Manipulation and Catastrophe Prevention Unit. The members of this Unit at all times are the President of the United States, the Four-Star General of the U.S. Army and Space Force, the Lieutenant General of the U.S. Marines, the Admiral Chief of the U.S. Navy, and the U.S. General Air Force Chief of Staff.

Brigadier General Knight, the second you became aware of the existence of time travel, you were inducted into this unit. There are strict laws governing the use of time travel, and I expect you to familiarize yourself with them A.S.A.P. I attached another file to your watch for this purpose.

I had no idea at the time, but now I can only guess that the T.M.A.C.P.U. message was sent to me by a future version of myself—it's dated only a few weeks from today— which means that I'm going to be running into trouble really soon.

When I received the message twenty-five years ago, I assembled the T.M.A.C.P.U. We followed the order on the message. We investigated Tobias Knight and pretended to still investigate Staff Sergeant Knight for the sake of appeasing the nation's leaders, who had no knowledge of the message. We didn't find anything at first. Tobias led a completely normal life—for a genius scientist. For years we almost convinced ourselves that he was innocent. But the message from the future couldn't have been a mistake. We kept investigating.

In 2232, Tobias began to lose his memory. He faltered for long minutes when he gave talks and speeches around the world. Sometimes, he wouldn't even recognize his own family.

In 2238, Tobias was admitted to the permanent psychiatric ward at Providence Saint John's Hospital. The doctors couldn't figure out what was wrong with him. We became ever more doubtful that Tobias was the source of the virus. He came up clean everywhere we looked.

It took years of digging. We had to track down old friends, who were few, and family, who were all dead. The clues finally led us to what we were looking for.

In 2241, we discovered Tobias's secret lab. In it, we found documents that revealed that he experimented with cloning and the creation of human-friendly viruses, both of which activities are illegal. In addition, we discovered underdeveloped relatives to the benign virus that now plagues us. There were detailed design plans and manuals for Liao Inserts. That's how he did it—he hacked those systems and programmed them to construct the virus directly inside the body. Those who had Inserts, which was nearly everyone, had the virus. Those who didn't were virus-free. We suspect that he gave it to Brigadier General Knight directly.

It was certain that Tobias Knight created the virus and infected the human race with it. We didn't know its purpose at the time, but it couldn't be anything good considering the message from the future. The option of revealing our investigation to Tobias and interrogating him was lost due to his illness. So we had to go on what we had.

We confiscated everything from Tobias's old lab and began studying the materials. Someone came up with the idea of putting the old virus into an isolated time machine. It doesn't actually send anything through time but speeds up or slows down time only within the space of the machine. When the virus had experienced a simulation of thirty years, it began destroying human cells.

We don't know why Tobias did this—we can't question him now—but he has attacked the entire human race. He is now facing charges of treason and conspiracy. It won't do much good—he won't even know that he's been caught.

There is, as yet, no cure for his invention. Everyone on the planet may very well die if a solution isn't found.

THE LEGEND OF THINGS PAST

Brigadier General Knight, you were selected for this mission because you know your grandfather better than anyone. The two of you were very close before he became sick. We're hoping that you will have an edge, will have insights into the way his mind works. We sent you back to find Tobias in his right state of mind.

If he has already created the virus, then you are to interrogate him and discover the potential whereabouts of a cure, or, failing that, you are to stop him from creating it in the first place—at all costs.

Succeeding at this, you will return to your proper time period.

I know this will be hard for you, Donovan. This is the reason I made you accept the mission before telling you about it—I was afraid that you would not agree. I would have gone myself, but I already exist in the year 2180—in fact, I should be a Colonel in the A.S.F. I can't risk running into myself.

You're the best we've got. This is for the sake of the world—don't forget that.

Find a cure, Donovan, or the human race will become extinct.

Chapter 5

"Quis custodiet ipsos custodes?"
"Who will guard the guards themselves?"

—Juvenal

May 4, 2176
Fort Belvoir, VA
Donovan Knight

With shaking hands, Donovan hit the stop button to prevent the brief from playing all over again. His insides had turned to mush. He felt like he was going to vomit.

How could this be happening?

There was no way this could be real. It had to be a setup. There had to be a reasonable explanation. The Tobias he knew was strict, maybe even ruthless at times, but this was ridiculous. To say he was a psychopath out to destroy the human race was just... crazy. The grandfather he knew wanted to help the human race, not destroy it. Maybe the whole thing had been an accident. Maybe the virus was meant to help people but had gone wrong.

Donovan stared into his lap.

Breathe. Stay calm. Don't panic. Think objectively.

After a few long minutes of complete silence in which General Umar just looked at him, Donovan spoke.

"I'll agree to investigate my grandfather," he said. "But I'm not going to hurt him. He's going to tell me the truth. Then this whole charade will be over."

General Umar didn't respond to his words. His face said that he thought it would do him no good.

"I'll have you escorted to your quarters now. You can review the laws of time travel and get some rest. If your mind will let you. We'll reassemble tomorrow and decide what to do."

General Umar pushed a button on his desk. A voice came through some hidden speaker.

"Yes, General Umar?"

"Will you please escort Brigadier General Knight to his quarters?"

"Yes, sir."

The speaker turned off with a click. "He doesn't know where you're really from. No one does except me. Everyone here has been led to believe that you're an Army Specialist from this time period brought in to help on a special case. They don't know what the case is about, but they know it's important enough that you teleported directly into my office."

The General pointed into the corner. There was a narrow tube large enough to fit one person. It was teleportation machine. It looked much like the time machine that was hidden in the wall.

"Keep your watch on. I need to be able to communicate with you at all times."

General Umar gave Donovan his phone number and told him to memorize it.

"Yes, sir." More than anything Donovan just wanted to get out of there and have time to think to himself.

The Private, whose name Donovan was too preoccupied to remember, led him to what would be his room for however long it took him to meet with his grandfather and get the necessary information out of him. He didn't expect that it would take long. In 2176, his grandfather was fifty-four years old—already a well-known scientist for having created teleportation in 2157. It was odd to think that he was older than his own grandfather.

The government had already recruited Tobias so Donovan would have no problem finding where he lived. It was just a matter of knowing how much he could tell his grandfather without breaking any time-traveling laws.

The Private sent Donovan's room key to his watch. Donovan waved his wrist over the scanner under the doorknob and it beeped green, unlocking.

"You'll find that you have rather extensive accommodations, fitting someone of your rank. There is a map and directory of the base inside your desk drawer."

"Thank you." Donovan quickly dismissed the Private, assuring him that he didn't need any assistance.

When he was gone Donovan went straight for the twin bed in the right corner, which was unusually comfortable. He lay on his back and stared at the smooth white ceiling. It was his habit to thoroughly examine his living quarters when on a mission—get settled into the place, check out the base if he hadn't been there before—but right then he needed quiet. He needed to lay there and do nothing.

He still couldn't truly believe that his grandfather was at fault. He played through the brief again, letting the facts run through his mind:

They had found an older version of the virus in Tobias's lab.

They found other human-friendly viruses, the purposes of which they didn't know.

They found design and operation manuals of Liao Inserts.

They found various paraphernalia indicating that his grandfather had experimented with cloning.

These were the facts, but what did they mean? Certainly, they were suspicious. Certainly, they required some type of government punishment, but had they fit all the clues together accurately?

Yes, maybe his grandfather did create the viruses, but did that mean for sure that his intent was to destroy the human race? Wasn't it possible that he had created the virus to cure common illnesses? To strengthen the human body rather than harm it?

So what if the virus had turned bad. Didn't intent matter?

But what about the manuals?

So what? Donovan thought. It could be a coincidence. It didn't show beyond reasonable doubt that his grandfather programmed the world's Liao Inserts to infect them with the virus. General McGregor just had a bunch of dots that he was trying to force together because of the message he'd gotten from the future.

The only thing Donovan could see that his grandfather was guilty of was cloning and negligence. It would earn him a long prison sentence for sure—but at least he wouldn't be guilty of treason.

Cloning and negligence Donovan could believe. It made much more sense than Tobias plotting to kill everyone on the planet. His grandfather was a zealot of a scientist. He was passionate about pushing limits, about discovering things that previous generations had thought were impossible. It was far more likely that he would break the law for the sake of discovery.

Donovan remembered his grandfather's fervor more than anything else about him. There were times when Donovan was a boy when Tobias had given him lessons and Donovan had suddenly thought that his grandfather was slightly insane. The memory came through in a flood.

***

"And what is the logical conclusion? If we cannot disassemble the atoms and reconstruct them elsewhere? What do we do?"

The thirteen-year-old Donovan stared at his grandfather, willing the answer to him. Sometimes he wished he could see into his grandfather's mind and make copies of the information there for himself.

Tobias had a fire in his eyes that Donovan was all too familiar with—it was as if Tobias wished he could turn the cogs in Donovan's mind and make him come to the right conclusion.

Donovan often felt as if his brain was dusty, muggy even, compared to his grandfather's. The wheels in his mind were not properly oiled and would not work as smoothly.

Donovan ventured a guess. "Then we should..."

Tobias's eyes widened, an expectant expression on his face. He looked a touch crazy, as if he would lose his mind if Donovan gave him the wrong answer.

"...We should bend the space-time continuum, which eliminates the need to break down the atoms in the first place."

"Precisely, my boy! Precisely!" The look on Tobias's face was euphoric, like he'd come to some life-changing realization. He was so happy that it made Donovan laugh.

"That's it. I knew you could think of it on your own. You have my genes, my boy. No mistakes there."

Donovan grinned, proud of himself and grateful for his grandfather's praise.

"You could go far in the sciences you know."

"I don't know..."

"Of course you could! Do you know what you just accomplished here?" Tobias had a maniacal gleam in his eye. "You just discovered the secret to teleportation! On your own, at the age of thirteen."

Donovan just smiled and let his grandfather rant. He had yet to tell Tobias that he didn't want to go into the sciences—he wanted to join the army, like his father. Donovan wasn't sure he'd ever work up the courage. For now, he just let Tobias shove information into his brain.

"Granted," his grandfather continued, "you did have me to help you. But there are plenty of adult physicists who can't figure this stuff out with or without help. I think my genius skipped a generation. Your father wasn't very much good at this."

Donovan became still and his smile faded a little. *Here we go.*

"He joined the army to be a *weapons specialist*. As if that would do any good for the world."

Donovan had heard this story a million times.

"He was smart. I know he could have gotten it, had he just tried, but he was lazy up here." Tobias pointed to his temple. "All he wanted to do was shoot people. Completely uncivilized. Complete waste of talent."

"Maybe he just wanted to fight to protect people," Donovan said, surprising himself.

His grandfather gave him an odd look. "He just wanted to hold a gun and feel powerful. He could have saved people with science."

"Maybe that just wasn't his way of helping. Maybe he was meant for something else."

The way Donovan said it must have triggered Tobias's suspicion.

"Are you having doubts?" he asked. "Do you want to join the army like your father? Specialize in guns and fighting?"

Donovan didn't answer. He glared at his grandfather.

"You do remember that it was being an army specialist that killed your father, don't you?"

Donovan shrugged. "He died a hero."

Suddenly, Tobias was on his feet. "He died a fool!"

"Not everyone can be a genius!" Donovan snapped back. "Not everyone was meant for this."

His grandfather was breathing as if he had just run a marathon.

Donovan glared back at him. With something close to desperation he said, "Not everyone can be like you."

Tobias stared at Donovan as if he'd been struck—but he wasn't really looking at him. Donovan stepped off his stool and took a step forward.

"Grandpa?"

Tobias's eyes came slowly back into focus. His breathing calmed and he began to nod his head as if answering an unspoken question.

He looked at Donovan as if seeing him for the first time. "Perhaps not."

With that, he turned his back on Donovan and left the room.

***

At times like those, Donovan had feared that his grandfather's mind was unstable. He could become so angry so quickly then become calm just as fast—like the anger had never been there at all. It left Donovan feeling tense—waiting for his grandfather's temper to explode. It didn't always happen, but when it did it was always related to science and was always unexpected. But Donovan refused to believe that this made Tobias a criminal.

Most of the time, his grandfather had been normal, kind even. He would take Donovan to visit slum cities and give out food to the homeless. He initiated government programs and non-profit organizations that would brought better education to the poor cities that still littered the country. And on some days, when he wasn't being a genius or a philanthropist, he was an ordinary grandfather and took Donovan out for ice cream.

Donovan had loved those times, when his grandfather gave him his full attention. There were no lessons, no scientists, no government officials—just the two of them. They had gone to the duck pond near the Santa Monica Square and fed the birds while they licked their desserts. In the summer it was always a beautiful environment—the crisp blue water, the cloudless sky, the many-colored kites that hung in the air, the chirping of birds, the quacking and waddling of the ducks, the laughter of families having a good time together.

It was amidst all this that they would sit in the grass at the edge of the pond and talk. They would talk about everything from what Donovan was learning in school to what his friends were like, and what area of science he liked the most. In turn, his grandfather would tell him stories about their family—everyone was dead by then, except the two of them. Donovan had never met his grandmother and he was starting to forget his memories of his own parents, so he would always ask a ton of questions about them. He didn't want his memories to fade completely. He needed his grandfather to keep them alive in his head—otherwise it would be like they never really existed. And then who would Donovan be?

Who were his parents, really? What were they like? Were they nice people, good people? What had been his father's favorite flavor? Did he like spicy food? Did he enjoy rollercoasters? Were his parents really in love? Did they really love Donovan? Why did his mother have to die too? What did it mean to die of grief? Didn't she love him enough to stay?

Tobias had patiently answered his questions, putting an arm around Donovan's shoulders. He had assured Donovan that his parents loved him very much, that his father had loved spicy foods and that his favorite flavor was caramel. He loved roller coasters. Donovan's parents had been in love since the day they'd met.

Some questions were not so easy to answer. Sometimes, all Tobias had to give was a simple, "I don't know, son."

"Your parents were good people," Tobias had said one day at the pond. "They cared about others—about helping them. I never agreed with them about how to go about it—but, still their intentions were true. You see the beauty of this world, Donovan?"

Donovan had nodded, looking at their surroundings.

"We almost destroyed it once. But we used science to fix it."

Donovan knew this—everyone did.

"This world could be a utopia, but it isn't—humans are still humans. Without a world to destroy, we'll destroy ourselves. The next step in science is to figure out a way to save humans the way we've saved Earth."

Donovan had thought it was a beautiful notion—saving humans from themselves. But now, as he stared at the ceiling of his room at Fort Belvoir, he had to wonder, who would save the saviors?

Donovan dragged himself away from the memories of his grandfather to focus on the present. *How was he going to clear his name?*

Donovan pulled up the second file General McGregor had attached to his watch. *The Laws of Time Travel.*

Too tired to read through it all, Donovan hit the audio button. A simulation of a human voice emanated from the watch.

The laws writ herein shall be the sovereign law of temporal manipulation in the United States of America.

No individual or organization shall own a temporal manipulation unit outside the express permission of the T.M.A.C.P.U.

There shall be no messages sent through time except in states of extreme emergency such as nationwide or worldwide catastrophe.

There shall be no persons sent through time except in states of extreme emergency such as nationwide or worldwide catastrophe. A person or persons can only be sent through time if their presence cannot cause further harm to the future.

Only one person can be sent through time from any given point in time.

Only one person can be sent through time to resolve a specific issue. That person can only be sent once. If that person fails to resolve the issue that he or she was assigned, the government may not send that person or any other through time to resolve the same problem.

Travelers shall not reveal their identities to any person in another time unless strictly necessary to the task they are assigned to complete.

Violation of these laws may cause irreversible and/or irreparable damage to history.

Violators shall be punished to the fullest extent of the law.

Well, that seemed simple enough. Don't mess with time unless the world's going to end. Don't tell anyone you're from a different time period. Easy.

Except the fact that it would be difficult for Donovan to get any information from his grandfather without revealing who he was. He'd get very little from Tobias as a stranger, but if Tobias knew that Donovan was his future grandson.

But the law was clear. It had to be strictly necessary. Donovan could probably get what he wanted without letting his grandfather know—it would just be more challenging.

Donovan rubbed his eyes. He was exhausted from the trip in the time machine. Adding the stress of finding out that the government suspected his grandfather of attempting to kill off the human race made his eyes droop heavily. He wanted to go to sleep, but his mind wouldn't stop racing. All he could think about was how he was going to talk to his grandfather. What approach would he take?

Nothing came to mind.

Donovan's stomach growled and only then did he realize that he was starving. He got up and stretched. He readjusted his watch. He had followed the technological development of watches for the last twenty years, buying new models each time they came out. He had watched them phase out in favor of the more personal capabilities of Liao Inserts. No matter how normalized Liao Inserts became, Donovan couldn't talk himself into getting them.

The halls of Fort Belvoir were much the same in this time as they were in the future—long, narrow, and full of slide show pictures of long-dead military women and men. Standard industrial carpet lined the floors.

Donovan followed the path that would lead to the cafeteria eighty-two years from now, wondering if it had stayed in the same location all those years. It had, but it would clearly be remodeled at least once before 2258 came around. The one in the future was full of stainless steel surfaces and black granite table tops. This one still had wood tables and chairs.

On one side of the room there was an old-school-style food-serving area. People lined up with trays and the staff behind the counter scooped the food out of deep dishes and plopped it onto their plates as they passed by.

On the other side was a full menu hanging from the ceiling and a counter where you placed your order. Then the cooks made your food fresh. Donovan headed in that direction, not too intrigued by the options he saw in the tray line.

The cafeteria was just as crowded then as it would be in Donovan's time. All the tables were full and the kitchen staff moved at a feverous but controlled pace. Donovan wasn't sure how the meal plans were structured in 2176, but he knew he'd have free food while he was here, so he didn't bother trying to find out.

Donovan stepped into line behind a man with brown hair. He was average height and, from his uniform, Donovan could tell he was a Captain. When the man sensed Donovan come up behind him, he turned around and gave him a friendly nod.

When Donovan was next in line, still pondering the menu, wondering what was good, someone spoke from behind him.

"You should go for the barbeque burger. It never fails."

Donovan turned around to see a stunningly attractive woman. She had on a blue vest over a white t-shirt and a pair of fitted black pants. Everything she wore had dozens of pockets. She was tall, and her muscles were clearly visible through her clothes.

Donovan smiled at her automatically, eyes drawn to her smooth brown skin and almond shaped eyes. Her black hair was cropped short, stopping around her ears and had dark blue streaks running through it. Instantly, Donovan was reminded of some jungle cat like a tiger, something both powerful and beautiful. The way she held herself, so balanced, told Donovan that she was probably a good fighter.

"Is that so?" Donovan asked. "I think I'll give it a try. Thanks for the recommendation."

She smiled, flashing perfect white teeth. "No problem. I'm Tracee Parker by the way. Brigadier General. Army Specialist."

Donovan's smile widened. "Well, what a coincidence." He shook her proffered hand. "I'm also a Brigadier General and Army Specialist. Donovan Knight."

"Oh!" She seemed surprised. "What brings you to Fort Belvoir?"

"A special case. Can't talk about it."

"Ah, I see," Tracee said.

By then it was Donovan's turn to order. He followed Tracee's recommendation.

As he took his order number, she said, "You won't regret it." She winked at him.

Donovan's extremities tingled. He smiled. "Thanks a lot."

He sat down to wait for his food, played around on his watch, and looked at Tracee out of the corner of his eye. She was interesting to say the least. He wondered how strong she really was, what her specialties were. When she turned in his direction he quickly redirected his gaze back to his watch, pretending to scroll through some articles.

When he looked back up she was talking animatedly to another soldier. She was still chatting with him when Donovan's order was up—they seemed to know each other well. He retrieved his food and sat back down. He had planned to eat in his room and go to sleep, but he didn't feel so tired anymore.

Tracee was still talking to the other solider when her own order was ready. Donovan watched her grab her food and walk in his general direction. His chest expanded. He looked down at his plate and took another bite. When he looked up again, Tracee had passed his table and was headed out the door.

The little bubble in his chest burst, leaving him feeling disappointed. He ate the rest of his meal without distraction then returned to his room. As he lay on the bed, eyes closed, waiting for sleep to overcome him, he thought of his wife, her soft form and how she would be wondering where he was.

He had never called her back. Would the General contact her? No, probably not. He'd said that if Donovan was successful... then he'd never be sent on this mission in the first place. He would change the future. His mind bent at the thought of it.

If he stopped his grandfather from programming the Inserts with the virus—if, in fact, that's what he'd actually done—then he would never get the virus and neither would anyone else. He would never get the strange news after his first physical when he joined the army. The army would never quarantine his house, would never scare his children. In the future, after leaving his grandfather's hospital room, he would go back to his wife.

A thought occurred to Donovan and he sat bolt upright.

What will happen to me? The me who's sitting right here, right now?

There would be no future for him to go back to. If he changed everything and was never sent to Fort Belvoir, then there would be two of him when Donovan returned to 2158. Unless... Donovan's brain seemed to twist in his skull, trying to grasp information just out of his reach. He tried to remember everything his grandfather had ever told him about time travel.

Then it came to him. If he was successful on this mission, this version of himself, the flesh and blood person sitting there, would disappear as if he'd never really existed. It would be as good as being dead.

Suddenly, Donovan felt trapped. The room felt too small and he couldn't breathe. There wasn't enough air in there for him to draw breath. He got out of the bed and stumbled to the floor, the energy gone from his body.

He understood that he was having a panic attack and crawled to the bathroom. There had to be a paper bag in there somewhere. He found one in the cabinet under the sink and opened the top, fingers fumbling. He breathed into the bag, his chest rising a falling rapidly.

You're still alive. You're still alive.

After a few moments, he calmed down and wiped the sweat from his face with the sleeve of his shirt. He walked back to the bed and collapsed onto it. He made a concentrated effort not to think too deeply about the consequences of this assignment. He shuddered, feeling weak.

No more thoughts came to him as he lay there. He slipped into a stupor, mind blank with fatigue. He fell asleep almost immediately.

Chapter 6

"And above all, watch with glittering eyes the whole world around you because the greatest secrets are always hidden in the most unlikely places."

—Roald Dahl

May 5, 2176
Fort Belvoir, VA
Donovan Knight

Donovan awoke to the sound of a bell. It was his watch. It was ringing. He had slept soundly, with no dreams. It was the kind of sleep that went by quickly—when he woke up he wasn't immediately aware that it was the next day. For a moment he was surprised to see that he was not in his own bed. Then the events of the previous day flooded his memory. A sinking feeling dripped into his stomach.

Donovan closed his eyes again, not yet wanting to face the day. Finally, he answered his watch.

"Brigadier General Knight." Donovan recognized the voice of General Umar.

"Yes, sir?" The remnants of sleep colored his voice.

"Report to my office at 1300 hours. You have five clean uniforms waiting for you outside your door."

"Yes, sir."

"I need you focused, Knight. See you in twenty minutes."

Donovan hung up and let his arm drop by his side. He sighed. He didn't want to do this. He didn't want to save the world if it meant he would lose himself. He wished he hadn't been so quick to accept this assignment without having more information. He had trusted General McGregor too much. He would never have expected him to do this.

Donovan had said he was ready to sacrifice everything, that he was willing to die—and he was. But not like this. It would be okay to die if his wife and children remembered him. This wasn't anything like that—he would just disappear as if he'd never been and then no one he cared about would remember him at all.

There would be a whole different copy of himself in the future, completely different from who he was now. In a sense, it wouldn't even be the same person.

Donovan dragged himself from the bed and into the shower. He stretched under the water, working out the tight kinks that had formed in his neck and back. When he was clean he cracked the front door and spotted a white cloth bag. He tugged it inside and shut the door. Just as General Umar had said, it contained five identical uniforms, each signifying his rank with a blue and white striped pin and a gold star.

He pulled on the uniform and checked his appearance in the mirror. He stared into his own blue-grey eyes, which looked tired.

You're going to die.

The morbid thought was unexpected and he banished it from his mind. He pocketed his watch and left the room.

Donovan walked into General Umar's office at exactly 1300 hours. A group had already assembled there. The first person he noticed was Tracee Parker, the woman he had met yesterday. He was both surprised and pleased to see her there. Maybe he would get to learn more about her. He was eager to test his own skills against hers. He hadn't met very many female army specialists before.

She gave him a small smile and a wink, a lock of blue hair falling in front of her face. She pushed it back with a flip of her head. Only after he had taken her in did he observe the others in the room.

There were three men, all with the rank of Lieutenant. One had bright red hair and looked very young to be a Lieutenant. Freckles dotted his small nose. Another had electric blue eyes and jet black hair that fell around his ears. He ran his fingers through the curly locks, pushing the hair out of his face. The last was short with brown hair and a large nose. They were all very muscular and fully loaded with weapons. They had the full range of e-guns, from stunners to rapid fire lethal shot guns.

There was also another woman, of the same rank as the men. She was equally as fit and carried the most lethal weapons of the group. Her dark brown hair was cut perfectly even and hung just above her shoulders.

General Umar sat behind his desk.

"Welcome, Brigadier General Knight. Now that you're here we can get started. Everyone take a seat."

There were folding chairs spaced out at regular intervals around the General's desk. Donovan sat in the middle. Tracee sat next to him. General Umar introduced the rest of the assembly. The redhead was Jonathan Chaplain, the blue-eyed man, Eric Kirk, and the short man, Blaise Contreras. The woman was Paula Kingston.

"Donovan, would you please play the brief for us?"

"Yes, sir." He removed the watch from his wrist and laid it flat on the General's desk. Donovan tapped the play button of the brief's audio.

He leaned back in his chair and stared at General Umar's desk as the horror of the brief played all over again. He felt sick to his stomach. When it was over he looked up. Everyone was looking at him. General Umar cleared his throat.

"Well, you've heard it. Donovan Knight is an Army Specialist from the year 2258. This is a mission that needs to be completed with the utmost secrecy. You will have your headquarters here, on the fifty-fifth floor. I may add or remove members of this team as necessary."

"So wait," Tracee said, "time travel..." she was shaking her head.

"Yes," General Umar said. "It's real. It was invented some years ago. Of course it cannot be public knowledge. No one can know that this technology exists. Our job is to complete the mission while assuring the stability of time. Everything must remain the same."

With a look a Donovan he added, "Or mostly the same."

Donovan was startled out of his dejected mood. So General Umar had thought that far ahead. He knew what this would cost. Donovan wondered if the others had realized it yet.

Probably not. They were still trying to wrap their minds around the idea of time travel, let alone its implications.

"Parker, you'll be in charge of all the travel details of this mission. You will be the pilot of all vessels. You will also act as a guard for Knight in cases of combat."

Donovan shot him a displeased look.

"Not that he needs it," the General added. "The rest of you will serve as backup for Knight. You are to help him conduct searches and, if necessary, you will help Parker to defend him. Protecting his life is a priority. If he's killed, our number one link to Tobias is lost. We'll lose our edge. Is that understood?"

"Yes, sir," they all said in unison.

"Your first assignment is to conduct a search of Tobias's home. He just left town for a business trip in China. He does have surveillance in his house. You'll need to destroy any evidence that you were there. I'll be sending you his address. Approach from a distance. You're dismissed."

They filed out of the room. Tracee took the lead and gestured for them to follow her. They crowded into the elevator in the hall outside and went all the way to the basement.

The basement was where Fort Belvoir kept its fleet. There were skycars, skycycles, jets, and space craft. All state-of-the-art vehicles and vessels. Tracee led them to a small jetcar. It was a mix between a skycar and a jet plane. It was slightly larger than a skycar but had the speed and comfort of a jet. The sleek metal was a shiny silver but had blue stripes along the short wings. Tracee pressed the button on her key and the jet beeped, much like a skycar would. A set of stairs lowered to the ground from the right side.

The inside was all leather and pinewood surfaces. There were two seats up front—for the pilot and copilot. Tracee sat in the pilot's seat. Paula took the copilot seat. The rest of the crew took seats in the back, each of which like a comfortable leather chair nailed down to the floor of the jetcar. The seatbelt reminded Donovan of a child's car seat. One strap came from each side to buckle in the middle. Some inner mechanism pulled the belt tight across his chest, keeping him securely in place.

Tracee turned on the engine and stood to face the rest of them.

"Listen up," she said. "While you're on my aircraft, you are to follow my orders at all times. In the event that I should become incapacitated, the copilot will take over."

Eric smirked. "We're only going to search a house. It's not like we're going into battle."

"If Tobias is capable of infecting the human race with a deadly virus, then who knows what else he's capable of?" Tracee gave the man a stern look. "We have no idea what defenses he has in his house. We have no idea if this will escalate. We'll aim to make this go as smoothly as possible, but in the event that our plans fail, we need a chain of command in place while aboard this vessel."

"Yes, but..."

"That's enough." Tracee's eyebrows dipped low in a forceful warming, "That is the chain of command while aboard my jetcar. While on the ground, Brigadier General Knight will take the lead and I will be second in command. Is that understood?"

Something in the way Tracee stood, staring Eric down, made him shut up and nod. Donovan was impressed. He felt that tingling in his extremities that was becoming all too familiar.

When Tracee turned her back, the other guys fell into silent fits of laughter. Eric's ears turned red.

Tracee took the pilot's seat and raised the aircraft from the ground. It floated gently around the basement, passing all of the other vessels as it looped up and around. Finally, they came to a huge slot in the wall that led outside to ground level.

Tracee flew the jetcar straight ahead, picking up a massive amount of speed all at once. Donovan was almost afraid that she would knock off a mirror as they sped through the narrow opening. The jetcar made it safely out and within seconds they were in the air, soaring above Fort Belvoir.

Tracee put his grandfather's address into the navigation system. Donovan wasn't sure where his grandfather lived in this time period.

"Where are we going?" he asked.

"Atlanta, Georgia."

The trip didn't take long. Within an hour they had crossed the border into the state. Tracee landed just outside the city, right at the edge of the forest. She turned on the Mirage Builder installed on the vessel, and it blended into its surroundings. To any passerby there was nothing more there than trees, grass, and birds.

They walked the additional mile into the city using the navigation system on Tracee's watch. Once they reached the first tall skyscraper, Tracee came to a halt.

"Tobias's home is not far—about a mile southwest. From here, we'll head to the nearest rental skycar place. We'll rent a vehicle and disguise it with the Mirage Builder on my watch. We're going to be in the renovation business today. Once that's done, we'll enter the target's house."

She glanced at Donovan when she mentioned the target. Everyone else was not so subtle—they all looked at him questioningly.

"What?" Donovan snapped.

"Well, this is your grandfather isn't it?" Eric asked.

"What's your point?"

"The point is," Paula said, stepping forward, "whose side are you really on? If you feel conflicted, we'd be more than happy to conduct this search without you."

Only in retrospect did his team's random glances in his direction and the whispers behind the hands become significant. He had been too preoccupied with thoughts of his existence to notice that his peers didn't trust him.

You're slipping Knight. Donovan could hear General McGregor's voice in his head.

"Look," he said. He looked each of them in the eye as he spoke. "I'm risking my life for this mission. What do you think will happen to me if we fail? That I'll go back to my time-skipping happy life because my grandfather managed to escape? My wife and children have this virus. When I left, my wife was already sick. If we fail, my family dies and so do I."

Donovan could see that they were less skeptical now. They were ready to trust him enough to follow him into enemy territory, even if they didn't trust him implicitly. But Donovan couldn't stop speaking, so caught up in the emotion of what he was saying. It was as if saying it out loud finally made it real.

"And if we succeed?" Donovan continued. "I still die. It'll change the future so that I was never raised by my grandfather—I'll be an entirely different person. In essence, the man who stands before you will no longer exist. So no one gets to question my loyalty. I'm screwed either way. But at least if we succeed my wife will still live. I may still meet her... She may still give birth to the same children."

Donovan realized that if he kept going his composure would break.

"No one gets to question me."

e stomped forward and they all stepped aside to let him pass. He didn't turn around to see if they had followed. He didn't care. He would get to the bottom of this whole fiasco with or without their help.

Moments later, he heard their footsteps behind him, crunching through the underbrush.

Donovan searched for the nearest car rental business and put the address in his watch's navigation system. They arrived within minutes. Tracee secured the skycar with the funds the military assigned to the mission. They flew to a deserted alley with no windows and made sure the coast was clear before using Mirage Builder to change the vehicle into a renovating team's skycar.

His grandfather's house was huge—the size of a small mansion. Donovan knew that his grandfather hated living up high in apartments. He hated sharing space with other people. In the future, he convinced the local government of Santa Monica to let him have his own property on the condition that he used his land to grow food. Apparently, he'd been doing that a long time.

Judging by the size of the place, they'd probably be there all day. The front of the house was styled much in the way of old houses that Donovan had seen in history books. It looked as if a mayor or senator had lived here in 2020.

There were four white pillars holding up the balcony that bordered the second floor. The porch was wide and held a rocking chair, a small table, and a hammock. Tons of potted plants and flowers littered the floor and the banister that ran along the front of the house.

Donovan crossed the yard, which was crowded with vegetable plants and fruit trees, and knocked on the front door. The others crowded around him with buckets of paint and brushes. He knew no one was there—he just had to do this in case anyone was watching—but he had an irrational fear that his grandfather would come to the door.

When no one answered, Jonathan stepped forward with his phone and held it up to the door knob. There was a click and the door creaked open. Donovan looked at him.

Jonathan shrugged and smiled mischievously. "I'm a tech specialist. I hacked his security system and programmed a renovation appointment for five minutes ago. The house has been expecting us."

Donovan felt ashamed—he hadn't even assessed the value of his crew before leaving. He had no idea who could do what. No wonder they hadn't trusted him. It looked as if he didn't care about this mission at all.

You have to get a hold of yourself, Knight. You have to focus. General McGregor's voice was clear in his head again.

Donovan took a deep breath and walked inside the house. The others marched in purposefully behind him, the sound of their footsteps and the swish of their clothes echoing in the huge space of the foyer. Someone closed the door.

They were in.

The foyer was a round room that led off to the other places in the house. To the left was the doorway to the kitchen. Next to that, an opening with a small set of stairs; they led into the living room. Directly ahead, a set of steep stairs curved up and away to the right.

To the right of the stairs were two closed doors. Upon opening them they discovered that the room next to the stairs was a rather extensive science library. They were all awed by it—libraries didn't really exist anymore. The next door led to a small room filled with leather chairs and solid wood tables. Another door inside the small study opened up to the library.

Donovan could definitely imagine his grandfather living very comfortably here. This would be paradise to him.

They began the search.

Everyone donned a pair of blue latex gloves. They used special military scanners to search for anything out of place—blood, hair, fingerprints. They wanted to know everything they could about Tobias—who kept him company in this large house when he got bored with the library, where he spent most of his time.

It was clear that Tobias spent many hours inside his library and the attached study. His fingerprints plagued the place, more so than in his own bedroom upstairs. The rest of the rooms in the house were cleared within minutes for lack of anything interesting.

They didn't find the lab spoken of in General McGregor's brief. But Donovan thought that might be because this was an entirely different house—maybe he hadn't built a lab in this one. Their scanners sensed no extra rooms—no extra security where there should be nothing.

They concluded that perhaps Tobias hadn't built the lab yet. If that were so, it would make it even more difficult to find clues. If he was using military labs for his private experiments he would clean up behind himself scrupulously.

They searched the library the most thoroughly, spending the bulk of their time there, trying to find helpful clues where there were none. The trouble was, they weren't exactly sure of what they should be looking for.

The shelves towered above their heads, reaching up to the full two-story height of the house. They were built into the walls, lined with book after book of every shape and size. The room had row after row of tall bookcases, all filled with books, old articles, or periodicals.

"Why does he have so many books?" Jonathan asked. "Hasn't he ever heard of an e-reader? They've been around for at least two hundred years."

"My grandfather hates virtual books. He says it's not the same as holding the real thing, feeling the pages."

Jonathan shrugged. "I suppose—I've never really read out of them to know. I haven't seen this many books all in one place though—how did he get them all? Do they have antique businesses that still print them?"

"No. Most people don't know it, but e-books come with a printing option. Usually only older people use it—and only the ones who have enough money to own a printing and book-binding machine."

"What's a book-binding machine?" Eric asked. Everything that came out of his mouth, even the most innocent of words, sounded belligerent. Donovan tried not to let his dislike for the man show in his voice.

"It binds the pages of the book to the cover."

"Ah." Eric didn't sound too impressed. In fact, he seemed somewhat amused by Tobias's oddity.

Donovan tried not to get angry. This was no time to go defending his grandfather over not liking the look on a man's face. They already suspected Donovan of being a traitor. If General McGregor were there, Donovan knew what he'd say.

Suck it up Knight. You're a solider, not a boy scout.

Instead of saying anything, he turned his back. He found Jonathan looking at him, almost knowingly—but when Donovan held his gaze Jonathan looked away.

The search neared its conclusion, and Donovan was beginning to feel as if they had hit a dead end. There was nothing there. They would probably have to bring Tobias in for questioning. Donovan both feared and relished the chance to talk to his grandfather face to face. Maybe then he could get the truth about all this. He was still sure that there had to be some kind of explanation. His grandfather had to be innocent.

As they were packing up their search technology and eliminating any DNA they left behind, Blaise climbed the ladder that allowed access to the upper shelves of the library. Out of all the crew, he had showed the most interest in the books, asking Donovan more detailed questions about how they were made. Donovan couldn't answer most of them, but that didn't stop Blaise from asking anyway.

Blaise stretched for a book a foot above the reach of his arm. He leaned to the left, fingertips grasping, his right foot leaving the rung of the ladder. Suddenly, he lost his balance. Donovan watched, knowing even as he rushed across the room that Blaise would take a hard fall.

The man tumbled to his left, arms flailing out madly in an attempt to grab onto something, anything. His fingers couldn't find purchase on the shelves. Books came plummeting to the floor as he groped for something to save him.

Unexpectedly, Blaise's fall halted. He had managed to catch on to one of the lamps that protruded from the walls at regular intervals. It couldn't hold his weight, however, and bent forward until it dangled upside down. The movement shook Blaise's grip and he fell—a much shorter distance—to land solidly on the floor.

The book shelves in front of Blaise began to shift. They slid to the side, revealing a dim passageway that turned sharply to the left.

It had happened so quickly that the others hardly realized what was going on until Blaise landed. They turned from their various tasks to see the pile of man on the ground looking up at them, still startled from his accident, and an opening in the walls that had not been there before.

Chapter 7

"A hero is an ordinary individual who finds the strength to persevere and endure in spite of overwhelming obstacles."
—Christopher Reeve

May 5, 2176
Atlanta, GA
Donovan Knight

"What the hell is that?" Paula asked.

"A secret passage, clearly," Tracee said, eyes trained on the spot. Donovan had not seen her remove her e-gun from the holster, but she now pointed it firmly in the direction of the opening, almond eyes wide as she concentrated on the spot. "Everyone stand back. Blaise get away from the door."

Blaise scrambled on hands a knees then stood up when he was a safe distance away. Tracee slowly approached the opening.

"Wait," Donovan said, reaching for her arm. "I'll go first."

"Your life is more important than mine right now," Tracee said without looking at him. "If there are any traps I'll find them. I go first."

"But..."

"That's my assignment," Tracee said. There was a little bit of anger in her voice. "I'm here to protect you at all costs. I go first."

Without waiting for an answer she walked purposefully forward and entered the darkness of the passage. The instant she stepped through, the corridor lit up. She approached the corner where it turned to the left and whipped around it, pointing her e-gun.

"Clear." She kept moving, disappearing behind the bend.

Donovan quickly followed her, drawing his own e-gun. Paula came up behind him and the rest behind her.

Around the corner was a long hall that sloped gently downwards and, at the end of it, a pair of doors. Tracee had already reached them, but she stood a couple of feet back.

"Chaplain!" Tracee shouted, keeping her eyes locked on the door and e-gun at the ready.

Jonathan rushed forward, the rest of them following closely.

"Here, BG Parker."

"I need you to open this door."

"Yes, ma'am."

Jonathan pulled out his phone and went to work. They all stood there, each passing moment increasing the tension in their muscles.

Finally, the double doors, which Donovan had presumed would swing open due to the fancy decorations carved into the wood and the shiny gold door hinges, slid to the side to disappear into the walls.

"Looks like we've found Tobias's lab," Tracee said.

"But how come my sensors didn't find it?" Jonathan said. He looked frustrated and fascinated at the same time. "They should have sensed a security system."

Donovan laughed.

"Don't you get it?" he said. "There is no security system. He didn't put one up because he knew that if anyone suspected him, they'd be looking for security systems to find hidden rooms."

Jonathan looked awestruck.

"I bet there wasn't even a lock on those doors. Tracee just assumed they were locked and you hacked into the sensor to force them open. But you didn't have to break through any security system did you?"

Jonathan's eyes opened wider. "I didn't..."

"Watch," Donovan said. "Close them again."

Jonathan did as he said. Donovan walked up to the closed doors. As soon as he was within a foot of them, they opened automatically.

"See?" Donovan said. "No security whatsoever."

"Wow," Jonathan said. "Never would have thought of that."

"Don't feel too bad. My grandfather is a genius, after all."

Eric sneered. "I suppose that makes you proud doesn't it? You sure you're not on his side?"

Donovan laughed again. "I'm not explaining myself again. Either you will follow me or you won't. Or, if you prefer, I can speak with General Umar and have you removed from the team. I'm sure he can find you a mission that has a leader more to your liking."

Eric glared at him and stormed past, brushing Donovan's shoulder.

Tracee looked at Donovan and winked. Then she followed Eric into the lab.

The entire room seemed to be made of metal. It was full of shiny, silver surfaces. There were multiple stainless steel refrigerators and tables. There was a deep sink and a long counter covered with test tubes, beakers, flasks, burettes, funnels, pipettes, and tons of other equipment Donovan didn't recognize.

It was clear that Tobias had cleaned the place meticulously—not a spill or a crumb anywhere, and every piece of equipment had its place.

Paula opened up one of the refrigerators. "Tons of test tubes in here. May be the virus."

"Take pictures and record each sample," Donovan said.

Paula nodded and got to work. She pulled out a black device with a small hole at the bottom. She placed the device over a test tube and pressed a button. A needle eased out of the hole and into the contents of the test tube. The device recorded the properties of the sample and the needle withdrew. Paula moved on to the next one.

The rest of them kept looking around, opening up cabinets and drawers. But there was nothing else interesting to be found. Tracee stood guard at the door, just in case they had unwittingly triggered some alarm that Tobias had hidden. Donovan doubted that there was any alarm system there, but Tracee insisted on being stationed at the door anyway.

Jonathan, Blaise, and Eric joined Paula in recording the contents of the test tubes. There were more of them inside the other two refrigerators. At least twenty test tube racks were inside each fridge and about ten test tubes to each rack. Donovan waited patiently for them to finish.

Just as they were wrapping up the last couple dozen test tubes, Donovan spotted a door in the corner, hidden behind a silver six-tier rolling cart. The shelves of the cart were packed with potted plants, which was why Donovan had not noticed the door behind it at first.

Donovan rolled the cart gently to the right to reveal a plain white door. The way it was wedged into the corner made him think it was a broom closet. Maybe this was where Tobias kept extra cleaning supplies.

Behind the door was not a closet but a whole other room, smaller than the first and filled with machines buzzing with advanced technology. Donovan checked on his team. Tracee was still just outside the front door—he could see the curve of her shoulder. The others had their backs to him, focused on the test tubes.

Donovan stepped cautiously inside. The thing against the opposite wall immediately drew his attention. How could he not look at it?

There was a wide counter and on top of it was what looked like a glass casket, like in that old Disney movie from the 2000s that his mother had made him watch. What was it called?

Snow White.

There was a body inside.

Donovan approached cautiously, slowly. What kind of sick operation was his grandfather running down here? Whose body was it? Donovan's breath came fast and he was afraid that the body inside the glass would move.

Donovan had the silly, irrational thought that his grandfather was experimenting with bringing back the dead. That couldn't be, because scientists had tried since the twenty-one hundreds and had reached a dead end in 2168.

Donovan knew because he had spent months and months after his parents' deaths studying the research, hoping against all logic that he could somehow spot a flaw in the experiments of the greatest minds in science.

Even his grandfather had told him it was impossible. If Tobias couldn't figure it out then no one would, but Donovan had tried anyway. He had only given up after an attempt to bring back a dead rabbit nearly killed him. Donovan had been surprised that he wasn't punished when his grandfather found out about it.

He'd never forgotten what his grandfather had said when he came to see Donovan in the hospital.

"Aren't I in trouble?" Donovan had asked when Tobias spent the whole visit without mentioning it. "I mean, I almost completely destroyed my room and I almost killed myself..."

"Shush, boy," Tobias had said gently. "There's no punishment for missing your parents."

Donovan has nearly cried, so happy that someone understood.

Knowing for certain that Tobias wasn't attempting to resurrect corpses, Donovan wondered if it was his father's body inside the casket. Looking intently at the figure from ten feet away—Donovan couldn't bring himself to go any closer—it did sort of look like his father. It had the same skin tone, the same angle to its nose, the same hands clasped at the waist.

Donovan took a deep breath.

It's just a dead body, Knight. Did I train you to be afraid of corpses? Get in there and investigate! Donovan wondered if General McGregor had implanted a device in his head to reprimand him whenever he messed up.

He took a step, then another. As he moved closer he realized that the figure was not his father. It was someone far more disturbing and confusing.

Inside the casket lay the body of world renowned scientific genius, Tobias Knight.

Donovan stumbled as he backed away. He fell hard to the floor, hitting his tailbone. He rubbed his back, scrubbing away the pain. Gingerly, he rose to his feet.

He heard General McGregor's voice in his head...

In 2241, we discovered Tobias's secret lab. In it, we found documents that revealed that he experimented with cloning and the creation of human-friendly viruses, both of which activities are illegal.

...and he realized that the body in the glass coffin—or not a coffin but a storage container—was a clone of his grandfather.

Much less afraid now, Donovan walked up to the glass. It looked exactly like his grandfather, from the hairs in his nose to the small mole on the left side of his neck. His eyes were closed. The clone was dressed in a suit. It really did look like a dead body. Donovan wondered how it worked—was the clone alive but in an artificial coma? Was it a working body with pumping blood?

As he thought the question, he noticed that the chest of the clone was rising and falling. So the thing was alive. But what was its purpose? Could it actually walk and talk or would it spend its life sleeping?

Maybe his grandfather had only created it to use it for its organs. Donovan shuddered at the genius of the idea. If Tobias's heart went bad, there was another, right there, working perfectly. All he had to do was take it. It was perfectly compatible. No rejection meds needed.

But then again, what about the life of the clone? Did it have its own personality, separate from Tobias? Did it have feelings? Or was it just a hunk of flesh to be used as a commodity?

Donovan stared into the familiar face, much younger than what he was accustomed to, but familiar nonetheless.

The hairs on the back of Donovan's neck stood up. He stiffened, certain that someone had snuck up on him and was standing right behind him. He listened closely.

Donovan heard the voices of his team in the other room. They hadn't noticed his absence—it had seemed like hours but he'd only been gone for a moment or two. They were talking about what they would do next. Donovan heard first Paula then Eric speak. Then he heard Jonathan. Where were Blaise and Tracee?

Certainly Tracee had to still be keeping watch? And even if it were her or Blaise, wouldn't they have said something by now?

All of these thoughts flashed through Donovan's head in a second. In one quick movement, he reached to his holster and drew his e-gun, spinning around at the same time.

He didn't even get to bring the e-gun up to eye level. A force like that of a charging bull knocked it out of his hand. He felt his bone crack as the gun went flying and fell to the floor.

Donovan shouted as the pain lanced up him arm, but he couldn't linger over it. He had to move or he would die. He was only aware of a hulking figure standing over him and the urgency of escape.

Instinct took over. Donovan grabbed the nearest object and held it in front of his face to block the next blow. As the fist of his attacker dented it, he realized that it was a large metal bowl.

The others had heard his shout and came rushing in. The man, distracted by the new arrivals, turned to defend himself. Donovan seized his chance. He grabbed his gun from the floor and stood up.

Paula and Eric had both already shot the man with the electric shock settings on their e-guns, but he was impervious to them. He charged forward and grabbed Paula by the throat, slamming her into the wall.

Donovan winced, knowing firsthand the strength of the enemy. A sickened feeling crept into his bowels as he saw Paula slide to the floor, blood trailing behind her head, eyes wide open. Donovan had seen that look in the eyes of many soldiers and even more enemies. She was dead.

The attacker had already moved on to Eric, who shot at the attacker over and over, fear making his hand shake. His volts missed every time.

Before Eric could react, the man had punched him in the stomach, sending him flying. Eric landed and did not get up. Blood began to spread on the stomach area of his white t-shirt. He lay on his side, staring at Donovan as blood dripped out of his mouth.

Donovan had never been this afraid in his life. There was no way anyone could be this powerful. Who the hell was this guy?

Jonathan and Blaise had retreated at the display of strength. They turned over tables and used them as shields, firing their e-guns over the top, settings on kill mode. Donovan added to their attacks, shooting at the man from behind, terrified that he would turn back around at any second.

Even the volts that landed did hardly anything to slow the man down. He shook momentarily each time he was hit but plunged forward relentlessly.

He reached over the table and grabbed Blaise by the shoulders. There was a gurgling noise as Blaise relieved himself. Donovan and Jonathan kept shooting. Only when Blaise was thrown to the side like a rag doll, body dangling over one of the tables, did Donovan wonder where Tracee had gone.

The man closed in on Jonathan. As if on cue, Tracee came running in from the main door.

"What happened?" she shouted.

"Where were you?" Donovan shouted at the same time.

Tracee saw the threat and immediately began shooting. Donovan kept up his fire. It didn't stop the man—or creature, Donovan was beginning to think—but it slowed him down enough for Jonathan to scramble backwards, out of its reach.

Jonathan would die if Donovan didn't do something.

You're going to die, a voice in his head said. *You're going to fail.*

Donovan leapt. He landed on the man's back and pulled his arms around the thick neck. He flexed his muscles, putting as much pressure on the throat as he could. If Donovan could hold on long enough, the man would suffocate.

Jonathan took his chance and escaped from the corner, running to stand beside Tracee.

The man struggled with Donovan, pulling at his arms. Each finger seemed to have the strength of ten men—the grip crushed Donovan's already broken arm. He ignored the pain and held on.

Deciding that he wouldn't be able pry Donovan from his neck, the man jerked his torso forward, flipping Donovan over his shoulder. The move was so fast and unexpected that Donovan let go and slammed into the table that held Blaise's unmoving form. It toppled on its side, sending them both to the ground.

In a second, the man was on top of him. Donovan heard shots being fired. He couldn't breathe. His brain was foggy. He was looking the creature square in the face for the first time. This creature—this man—who was he? It looked like...

"The e-guns aren't working on him!" Jonathan bellowed.

"I can see that!" Tracee yelled.

Donovan barely held off the man's efforts to reach his neck. The only thing that kept him fighting through the pain in his arms was the knowledge that, if he didn't, he would die.

"Tracee!" Donovan yelled. "Do something."

He could just barely see her over the man's shoulder.

Tracee dropped her e-gun then reached to her hip and pulled out another weapon.

She fired it. The sound of its explosion echoed around the room. Donovan's ears rang. He feared that his hearing might be permanently damaged.

For once, the creature halted for more than just two seconds. It seemed to feel the pain. It grunted and let go of Donovan, sensing that the bigger threat was behind him.

Tracee fired again. The creature's body snapped backwards from the force, but he stepped forward.

Then again and again she fired. The creature recoiled from the shots but then stumbled toward her, arms outstretched. Jonathan stood behind Tracee, mouth hanging open in a combination of terror and shock. If Donovan had had less control over his emotions and been less experienced, he would have looked the same way.

Finally, the creature swayed. In what seemed like slow motion, it collapsed face forward to the floor.

Tracee lowered her gun, breathing hard. Donovan got up, cradling his right arm. He bent to check Blaise's pulse. He was dead.

Jonathan stared at Tracee as she recovered her breath.

"How'd you...?" Jonathan stuttered.

"It's a gun," Tracee said through gasps. "A regular, old-fashioned gun. With bullets."

"A *gun* killed that thing?" Jonathan asked. "That's impossible."

Donovan took action. He took the sample recorders off Blaise then went back into the other room to do the same with Paula and Eric. He looked toward the glass coffin.

It was empty.

Donovan drew his e-gun again. "Tracee!" he said. If this clone was as strong as that man had been, he'd need her gun. She ran in behind him, weapon at the ready.

"What?" she asked. "What is it?"

But the room was empty.

Where had the clone gone?

"Nothing," Donovan said. "It's gone."

"What's gone?"

"Never mind that now. I'll tell you once we're all safely out of here."

"But what about this mess? We can't leave the place like this. He'll know we were here."

"We'll send someone later. He doesn't come back for another three weeks. For now we've gotta get out of here. You have the only working weapon."

Only then did Tracee seem to realize the danger they would be in if another enemy showed up. They each carried a fallen comrade out of the room and through the kitchen where there was a door that connected to the garage.

Tracee lowered Paula gently to the ground and went to fetch the sky car.

Donovan heard the garage door open and close. Only then did he open the door and carry Blaise to the skycar. They loaded the bodies into the trunk. Donovan wished they didn't have to do something so undignified, but it was the only way to return the bodies to the families.

They couldn't just leave them to rot.

Tracee flew them to the jetcar where they put the corpses into a secure icing unit in the back. It could hold up to five bodies. It would keep them preserved for up to seventy-two hours. At least the families could give them decent funerals.

Donovan had seen men die in awful, bloody ways. Sometimes there was nothing left behind but a single limb—a single arm or leg—to bury. The rest would have been turned to pulp or to ash by the enemy's weapon.

It was always really heartbreaking to see. The families would cry hysterically at the news.

There could be no viewing of the body. No final goodbyes. It would take a long time for those families to find closure. With no body to look at, how could they even reconcile themselves to the idea that their loved one had encountered death at all? Maybe this wasn't Denny's arm. Maybe they had gotten him mixed up with someone else.

But the DNA was always right. There was no room for error.

Donovan, Tracee, and Jonathan cleaned the blood from the trunk until there was no trace of it, even to their own scanners, then returned the skycar.

They walked back to Tracee's jetcar in silence, hearts heavy with what had happened in Tobias's lab.

When they boarded the jetcar and the door was closed, Tracee turned on Donovan.

"What happened in there?" she asked.

Jonathan looked from Tracee to Donovan, arms folded across his chest.

"I'd like to know that as well. One moment we were packing up samples, the next we were being attacked by... Well, I don't know what it was."

"What was that thing, Donovan?"

They were both skating around the one thing Donovan did not want to talk about—he had yet to have time to think about it himself.

"I don't know what it was. Clearly not human... Or more than human. It was my first time ever seeing it."

Tracee looked at him skeptically. "Are you sure you're on our side?"

Donovan was surprised that the question stung.

"Of course I am."

"But, come on, Donovan," Jonathan said. "The thing looked just like you."

So, at last, someone had said it out loud.

"I know that," Donovan said calmly. "Imagine turning to face an enemy that looks like it could be your brother. And then having that thing break your arm with a swipe of its hand, killing half your team with little to no effort and nearly strangling you to death!"

His voice had risen by the end. He got himself under control.

"I am not Tobias's side. I'm not sure what the hell he's doing, but I plan to figure it out. Don't forget what I told you— I'm screwed either way, but I'll be damned if I let my family die."

Tracee sighed. Her face fell into her hands. She rubbed her eyes with vigor.

"Okay, Donovan," she said. "We believe you. Tell us what happened."

Donovan told them how he'd spotted the hidden door and explored it. How he'd seen an exact clone of Tobias, how the man had attacked him from behind, how after the dust had settled the clone was gone.

"I don't know what to make of it. It's clear that Tobias was creating clones and I'm sure the records of the test tube samples will show that those were copies of the virus. But that thing... And the clone disappearing..."

Tracee shrugged. She sat in the pilot's seat. "Let's leave it for General Umar to think about. Everyone buckle up. Donovan, you take the copilot seat."

Donovan sat down, uncomfortable with taking over Paula's position so soon after she was killed. He felt awkward as he clicked the seatbelt home.

"Wait, but what about you?" Donovan asked, suddenly remembering. "Where did you go? You were supposed to be keeping watch."

"I was," Tracee said. "I went further up the hall. I thought if someone attacked I'd be able to hold them off until you guys were prepared to fight. I didn't know anything was wrong until I heard the tables crashing."

"I wish you'd been closer."

"Me, too," she said. "Then maybe the others would still be alive."

"That's not what I meant," Donovan said.

"I know. But I did."

They flew to Fort Belvoir in complete silence.

Chapter 8

"The great thing about new friends is that they bring new energy to your soul."

—Shanna Rodriguez

May 6, 2176
Fort Belvoir, VA
Donovan Knight

Donovan was trying not to see his grandfather as the enemy. It was all he could think about. Even as he had his arm repaired at Fort Belvoir's Hospital, even as he sat before General Umar that night giving his report, he still wanted to think that his grandfather was somehow innocent. Even after everything that had happened, he imagined something would reveal itself to clear Tobias's name.

Even after helping to the carry the bodies of his fallen comrades to the morgue, he still hoped to prove that his grandfather was guilt free.

Was he insane? Everything that they had seen so far showed clearly that Tobias was guilty. It didn't make any sense for him to be skeptical.

But Tobias was his grandfather—the man who had raised him. He wasn't perfect, but he couldn't be this twisted. Maybe the man they had fought was a clone gone wrong. Maybe that's why the door had been hidden, just in case anyone discovered the lab...

They were feeble excuses. Donovan knew it, but he held on to them.

General Umar had reacted to the news with a hard expression. He seemed to think the same as Tracee and Jonathan—Tobias was guilty. He dismissed them once the report was over, telling them he would think on the situation. He would let them know what he'd decided in the morning.

Donovan had returned to his room feeling especially gloomy. He stood under the hot shower water long after he was already clean. When he finally climbed into bed it was one o'clock in the morning.

Donovan awoke abruptly to a solid rap on his door. He checked the time on his phone, the bright glow stinging his tired eyes. It was six a.m.—an hour before he was due to talk to General Umar about the next steps on the case. He resigned himself to being tired that day.

"Just a minute," he yelled to the knocker. He pulled on pants and a t-shirt and opened the door.

It was Jonathan.

"Lieutenant Chaplain," Donovan said.

"Good morning, BG Knight." Jonathan didn't quite meet his eyes. He rocked back and forth on his heels.

"Um, good morning," Donovan said. "What is this about?"

"May I come in?" Jonathan raised an eyebrow.

Donovan stepped back. "Yes, sure."

"Thanks." Jonathan sat in the desk chair.

Donovan sat across from him on the bed. "What it is?"

"Well," Jonathan leaned forward, "I need to know something."

"Okay..."

"It's not that I'm prying or anything," Jonathan said. "And I know that you're a Brigadier General and I'm only a Lieutenant and I shouldn't be questioning you like this—I mean it's totally inappropriate..."

Donovan just stared at him, curious but too tired to react.

Jonathan took a shaky breath. "...but I need to know, if I'm going to continue on this case with you."

Donovan waited.

Jonathan looked down at his hands. "What are your intentions on this mission?"

"What do you mean?"

"I mean, I've been watching you and it's not hard to see that you're less than enthusiastic about this assignment. You got thrown into it unwittingly and the enemy is your grandfather. I've seen the look on your face every time someone says Tobias's name—every time they say anything negative about him. I can tell you want to defend him, but you can't. People will think you're a traitor if you do, but at the same time it's human nature."

Donovan was startled that this young redhead had seen so much just by looking at his face. He wasn't a Lieutenant for nothing.

You're slipping, Knight. Keep it up and you'll get yourself killed. You're lucky this kid is on your side. Donovan wished that General McGregor would just shut up now. He was tired of hearing his criticizing voice.

"My question is, Are you on this mission to prove him innocent or are you trying to find the truth?"

It was a good question. "I don't know. I've been trying to figure that out myself."

Jonathan gave him a look. He clearly didn't believe Donovan.

"I'm being honest here. I don't know. I've only been here for three days. Not a lot of time to process."

"Right." Donovan could tell that Jonathan was disappointed.

"Look, to be completely honest here... I wish my grandfather were innocent. I'm still trying to convince myself that he's innocent, that there's a mistake, that these are just experiments gone wrong. Everything is pointing toward his guilt. But this isn't just some man. It's impossible to be neutral. He's...he's..."

"Your grandfather. I get it."

"He's more than that. He raised me. My parents died when I was thirteen. Tobias is practically my father."

Jonathan looked at his hands again. "I'm sorry. I didn't know that. I didn't realize how close you—but of course you are. That's why they assigned you to this mission in the first place."

"Yes... Now you understand." Donovan was glad that Jonathan had come. He was young, but of all the people here he seemed to be the only one to get what was going on in Donovan's head.

He missed Nona now more than ever. He wished he could talk to her. Then he remembered that General McGregor had placed a very thorough gag order—even if he could see Nona he wouldn't be able to confide in her.

All he had right then was this redheaded kid.

"To answer your question, I'm here for the truth—but I don't necessarily want to hear it. If I can prove my grandfather innocent, I will. But I won't do or say anything deceptive to do it. If all of the things he's accused of are true, that makes him my enemy, no matter how much he did for me growing up. No one can mess with my family and walk away."

Jonathan stood up. "Thank you, BG Knight—for your honesty. I had to know before risking my life for you."

"I understand."

Jonathan helped himself outside. Before leaving, he turned around. He smiled, his eyes lined with sympathy.

"You're very brave, you know."

Donovan didn't know what to say. Jonathan closed the door before he could think of a response.

Donovan stared at the door, wondering over the conversation. He thought he'd just made a friend.

Donovan met with General Umar, Jonathan, and Tracee forty-five minutes later. Donovan was tired, but he didn't regret the conversation with the young Lieutenant that morning. He felt lighter.

He smiled warmly in Jonathan's direction. Jonathan smiled back.

General Umar looked at them. "You two having some kind of love fest over there?"

They snapped to attention, smiles wiped away in a second. "No, sir," they said in unison.

"Then take a seat and listen up. We don't have time for your bromance."

Tracee stifled a laugh.

When General Umar looked her way there were no traces of humor around her lips.

"I'm assigning Colonel McGregor and Captain Umar to this case. I think they have a certain skill set that will be helpful."

Tracee and Jonathan's expressions reflected the surprise that Donovan felt.

"But you can't assign him..." Donovan ignored General Umar's affronted look. "He can't know about his future self."

"Boy, do not tell me what I can and cannot do."

"But General..."

"Quiet!" General Umar said, leaning forward in his seat. "Do you think I'm an idiot? Do you think that an idiot would be in charge of the entire United States Army and Space Force?"

"No, but..."

"Then be quiet and listen."

Donovan swallowed the words on the tip of his tongue.

"As I was saying," General Umar continue, "Colonel McGregor is the most brilliant mind in technology that we've seen in recent years and Captain Brian, though lacking in serious combat skills, is the world's leading biologist. Both men are the best in their fields.

"Considering that we're going up against *the most intelligent man since Stephen Hawking*, I thought it would be a good thing to have the *best* working on this mission. Are there any objections to that?" It was clearly not a serious question, but Donovan couldn't shut himself up.

"But what about the time travel laws? No one is supposed to be able to have knowledge of a future self."

"Colonel McGregor will never know. We'll change the brief and sign it with a different name. If it doesn't allow you to edit we'll make a new one."

Donovan nodded. He felt a little uncomfortable at the prospect of lying to McGregor, even a younger version of him. He had to admit that they needed him though. Jonathan was good, but McGregor would be far more experienced.

"I've already briefed Captain Umar—he has a small team working under him but they don't know the true nature of the mission. He's at work analyzing the evidence you all brought back as we speak.

"I sent in another team to return Tobias's home to normal. They retrieved the body of the man that attacked you. Captain Umar is studying that specimen as well. We're hoping that when Tobias returns he'll attribute the disappearance of the thing to its own doing. However, that is unlikely, so we mustn't rely on that. We have to act as quickly as possible."

"Sir, what do we do in the meantime?"

"Get as much rest as possible until we get the results of Captain Umar's tests. Donovan, I need you to get to work on that brief. I'll summon you all when the results are in."

General Umar dismissed them.

Donovan returned to his room and opened up the brief on his watch. He tried to delete General McGregor's name from the document, but it didn't work.

There had to be an easy way to do this. He tried to copy and paste the document from his inventory to a Word document, but the watch wouldn't allow him to do that either.

Resigned, Donovan sat at the computer desk. He turned on the dictation feature and read the whole thing out loud. The computer typed up his words.

Now he had to figure out how to manipulate the audio to sound like someone other than himself and General McGregor.

He had no idea how to do it.

He called Jonathan who showed up to Donovan's room ten minutes later.

"Can you do it?"

"Yeah, it's easy." Jonathan grabbed the watch from the desk and started pushing buttons.

"Thank God. I need some sleep."

"Oh, sorry about that," Jonathan said. "I guess I came kind of early."

"It's all right, I needed it."

Jonathan used the computer to record the General's voice from the watch as it played the brief. Once the voice pattern was on the computer, he manipulated its essence so that it sounded like a completely different person. Then he applied the audio to the typed document.

"Now all we have to do is send it back to your watch's inventory." Jonathan stroked the keys. "There it is. Done. Just be sure to play the right one."

Donovan's watch beeped. He had a new email.

"Thanks man," Donovan said. "You're a genius."

"You'll think differently once you meet Colonel McGregor."

"I already have met him."

Jonathan laughed. "But he's a General in your time, isn't he? You've never really seen him at work with computers have you?"

Donovan scanned his memories. "No, not really."

"Then you may be surprised."

When Jonathan left, Donovan plopped onto the bed. He figured that a good nap was in order. He refused to stay awake thinking about the likelihood of his grandfather's treachery or the vicious murders of his day-long comrades. The best thing he could do was get some rest and be at his best when they resumed work.

Donovan fell asleep only to be woken by Tracee a few minutes later.

"Does no one believe in sleep in this place?" Donovan asked upon opening the door.

Tracee walked into the room without answering. She leaned against the edge of the desk.

"Sure," Donovan said. "Come right in."

"What did you tell Jonathan?"

"What?"

"To make you guys best buds," Tracee said sarcastically. "What did you say to him?"

"Why, are you jealous?"

Tracee stared at him.

"I didn't say anything to him. I mean, we had a conversation this morning." Donovan recounted what they had discussed.

He laughed. "Why is this so important to you? Why does it matter if we're friends?"

"I just—I thought—the kid is gullible. I just wanted to make sure you weren't filling his head with lies."

Donovan was stung. "So you don't trust me?"

"I'm not saying that," Tracee said.

"But it's true."

"I just didn't think your intentions were as pure as you tried to make them out to be. It was clear that you cared for your grandfather. I thought you might be in on it."

"Like I told Jonathan, I had no idea that this side to my grandfather existed."

Tracee nodded. "Good." She swiped a blue streak of hair out of her face then pushed off the desk, propelling herself to the door. "That's really good, because I like you. Wouldn't want to care too much about an enemy."

With that she left, leaving Donovan tingling.

Guiltily, he thought of Nona. He missed her so much and here he was getting giddy over some woman he had just met.

Tracee and I are only friends, Donovan said it to himself, but he felt like his wife was there, in his head, accusing him. *Just friends.*

He closed his eyes and rushed into unconsciousness, escaping the glare of Nona's beautiful brown eyes.

When the next knock came, Donovan was fully rested. It was three o'clock in the afternoon. He was needed in General Umar's office.

The room was becoming all too familiar to Donovan. Soon, he thought, he would have the whole place memorized in detail. He would be able to draw a perfect picture of it for someone who had never seen it.

General Umar was sitting at his desk, as usual, and another man sat with his back to Donovan.

General Umar looked up when Donovan walked in. "Ah, here he is. Brigadier General Knight, this is Colonel McGregor."

The man who would become the next leader of the U.S. Army and Space Force rose from his chair to shake Donovan's hand.

It was the strangest sensation. The man looked exactly like General McGregor except with all-black hair and less wrinkles. And there was—was that a smile?

Apparently the General wasn't always so poker faced. What had happened to make him that way in the future?

"Good to meet you, sir."

Donovan almost laughed. General McGregor had just called him "sir." He wasn't the General yet, but still, it counted. It definitely counted.

"Good to meet you as well. I trust that General Umar has brought you up to speed."

"No, actually, he's been very vague."

"Ah, well, let me clarify a few points. I have the brief for you right here."

They sat down and Donovan let the brief play.

After the Colonel had gotten over the initial shock, he composed himself rather admirably.

"I need you," General Umar said, "to be in charge of all communications involving this mission. Make sure they're secure. I will have the team in constant contact with the base. After yesterday's fiasco, I can't risk them being dark for that long. They need to be able to call for backup at a moment's notice."

"Yes, sir," Colonel McGregor said.

"I've already sent for the others. They should be here shortly."

A few minutes later, Tracee, Jonathan, and a man who looked a lot like General Umar entered the room.

The General invited everyone to sit, paying no particular interest to his son—Captain Umar had to be his son as they looked far too much alike. In fact, if not for their resemblance and the matching last names, Donovan would not have known they had even met each other before.

General Umar acted as if Captain Umar were just another soldier. Donovan supposed that was a good thing—fairness and all that.

"Captain Umar will tell us the results of his research."

Captain Umar cleared his throat. "Um, yes. Well, the results aren't looking good as far as any useful information. The man that attacked you wasn't a clone—it was a, well, sort of descendant, if you will."

Seeing their confused gazes, Captain Umar explained further.

"It has about 99 percent of his DNA. The other 1% is altered to make it look slightly different than Tobias. That was why the thing looked so much like you, BG Knight."

"So it's not some long lost brother of mine?"

"No," General Umar said. "Now, as for the test tube samples, they were exactly what we thought they'd be—the virus. Weak versions of them—but still rather dangerous. I have them secured in a vault.

"We couldn't figure out why the man was so violent. There were no markers in his genes. I think Tobias put it there specifically to guard that clone you saw. The fact that it disappeared convinces me even more. Tobias didn't want anyone to find it."

"So what do we do now?" Jonathan asked. "It seems that we're at a dead end."

Everyone looked at General Umar. He raised his hands, palms up. He shrugged. "I brought you all to this case because you have special qualities—certain abilities that give you more advantage than any other soldier in this building.

"I don't have the all the answers. It's up to you to figure it out. This is an elite mission—which means you'll have to put those elite skills to use. Put your heads together. The world is at stake."

General Umar got up and walked to the door. "If you'll excuse me, I have other matters to attend to. Someone has to keep this base running in working order. I'll leave Tobias to you. Report to me each morning and each evening."

He closed the door on them, leaving their brains to hum in panic, fear, and confusion. The world was on their shoulders. Donovan had no idea if they were smart enough to save it.

Chapter 9

For good ideas and true innovation, you need human interaction, conflict, argument, debate.

—Margaret Heffernan

May 6, 2176
Fort Belvoir, VA
Donovan Knight

Donavon sat in stunned silence with the others. Then all of sudden everyone was talking at once.

"We should just wait till he gets back from China," Tracee was saying. "Then we can bring him in for questioning."

"We need to use technology to our advantage," General McGregor said.

"I agree," Johnathan said. "We can use technology to spy on him. He'll never know that we're on to him. We can take our time and get as much information as we need."

"No, he's too smart for that, he'll figure it out," Captain Umar said impatiently. "We have to use a biological attack, like he is doing to us. I've been doing research on memory retrieval. There's a possibility that we could put him in an artificial comma and search his mind."

"Yes, but how far along is that research?" Jonathan shot back. "It's still in its infancy. We don't know for sure that it'll work. It could take years."

"But we have time," Captain Umar said. "This virus doesn't become a threat for another eighty-two years."

At the mention of time, Donovan spoke up.

"Quiet! Everyone, just be quiet!"

The room grew silent and everyone looked at him.

"I don't have time. I need to get back to my own time and I can't do that until this mission has succeeded or failed beyond any hope. I need to get back to my wife—if anything is even the same when this is all over."

Everyone had sober expressions.

"Now, what we need to do is not argue which of our ideas is best but find a way to put our talents together. We can't use old and tried methods. Tobias will be expecting that. We need something new—innovative. Something he doesn't even know exists. We need to become scientific inventors, like he is. That's the only way we'll be able to compete with him."

Tracee sat down with a *humph*. Jonathan joined her and stared at his hands, clearly thinking hard.

They sat or paced in silence for about thirty minutes before Captain Umar threw his hands up. "I've got nothing. This is impossible."

"It's not, we just have to think harder."

The clock ticked away the time. Someone would propose an idea and it would get squashed right away. Then another person would propose something else that seemed promising and they would toss is around for a while before deciding that it too was complete garbage.

"I've got it!" Jonathan jumped from his seat.

They all moaned. He had done this about a dozen times already.

"No, seriously guys, I've got it! What if we could create something that would trace the clone?"

"What are you taking about, you idiotic child?" Tracee asked, exasperated.

"The clone!" Jonathan said. His eyes bulged as if he'd go crazy if no one understood what he was talking about. "The one that Knight found in the lab. What if we could invent something that would track it? Figure out where it disappeared to. It could lead us to something."

They all shook their heads.

"What if Tobias didn't send the clone somewhere else?" Captain Umar asked. "What if he had a self-destruct setting on that glass case? Maybe the clone is gone—disintegrated."

"No," Donovan said. "Tobias would never destroy something like that. He's too vain when it comes to his work. It's very likely that it was teleported to another location."

Colonel McGregor nodded. "So in all likelihood he sent it somewhere else, but where? Maybe he has another secret lab somewhere. If we can figure out where that clone went. But how?"

"*HELLO!*" Jonathan said. "That's what I was just saying."

"Right," Donovan said. "Carry on."

"Captain Umar. Every person on the planet has a unique pattern of brainwaves, right? Similar to a thumb print?"

"Yes."

"And Colonel McGregor, there are machines that can sense brain waves, correct?"

"Yes."

Donovan's eyes widened in excitement as he realized where Jonathan was going. He sprang forward and scooped the redhead into his arms, spinning him around.

"You're a genius!" Donovan shouted. "A redheaded, freckle-faced little genius!"

The others were still looking confused.

"I'm not understanding...," Tracee said.

"How can you not see it?!" Donovan said. "It's absolutely brilliant! We invent a machine that can track specific brain waves. The brain of Tobias's clone will be exactly the same as his. It'll be a cinch."

"We may even be able to use the descendant we have here," Jonathan said. "If it has Tobias's DNA with a slight twist, it should be similar enough to help us track the other clone."

"That's..." A smile crept onto Tracee's face. "...Absolutely genius!"

Donovan turned urgently to Colonel McGregor. "Can it be done?" He looked at Captain Umar. "*Can it be done*?"

Captain Umar nodded. "It can be done... in theory."

Colonel McGregor's eyes were bright. "Yes, it could be done. It shouldn't be too hard. It'll take some excellent programming skills, but I think I can manage."

Donovan had never known General McGregor to brag about his talents.

Everyone was swept up in the excitement. They cheered and clapped. If they could really do this, they would save the entire human race from destruction.

They got to work immediately. Colonel McGregor and Captain Brian took of a corner of the fifty-fourth floor, building prototypes and drawing up plans for newer versions. They worked night and day, never leaving the room except to relieve themselves. Food was brought to them.

They set up partitions around their little corner. They would allow no one else inside and warned the rest of the team to stay away. They said that it would interrupt their creative flow. Donovan left the two of them to their work and distracted himself in the meantime. He went to the gym, he ran, he tried the many different food options at the base, he went for late night swims. When he was tired of his own company he would seek out Jonathan or Tracee.

They were both anxious to see the progress of the brain wave tracking machine. It made them all feel weird to be standing around doing nothing while Colonel McGregor and Captain Umar created the invention of the century.

To keep themselves from going crazy with impatience they hung out together. They discovered little nooks and crannies all over the base where they could be alone to discuss the mission. They usually talked in circles, saying the same old worn out words over and over again. They knew that it was useless, but at least it kept their minds busy.

They even started to meet up to think of new ideas. After all, there was no guarantee that the invention would work. Maybe they should have a backup plan. The meetings were fruitless as a rule, but they kept at it.

Tracee invited Donovan and Jonathan to train with her. They met in the gym in the wee hours of the morning and after a tough regimen of cardio, weight training, and stretching, they would enter the combat ring.

They would take it in turns, one person fighting another, and the winner taking on the spectator. Jonathan lost every time, no matter who his opponent was. Donovan and Tracee were evenly matched. Donovan was surprised the first time he fought her. She had jumped right in, landing solid kicks and punches to his chest and legs, bringing him down within seconds.

He lost that first fight out of carelessness. He had underestimated her. But from then on he fought with vigor—he would not go easy on her. Even when Donovan fought his hardest, Tracee still had the ability to beat him.

Donovan would spar with Tracee for hours, trying his best to win at least three matches in a row, but it never happened. Jonathan would often drop out of the competition early, easily wiped out by the two army specialists' workout routine. Jonathan was fit and a good fighter—but he was no match for either of them.

One day, after Jonathan had already headed for the showers, Donovan and Tracee faced off in the sparring ring. Each waited for the other to make the first move. Donovan had become accustomed to her style now—she was very aggressive, in contrast to his calm demeanor. He knew if he waited long enough she would lose patience and strike first. It never failed.

She lunged for him. He dodged to the side, grabbing her leg as it swung toward his side. She used his firm hold against him, twisting her entire body to bring the other leg up and around toward his face. Donovan dropped the one leg to block the other. A less skilled fighter would have lost her balance and fallen to the ground, but Tracee landed in a crouching position, on her feet. She sprang back up and struck again.

Donovan's mind went blank and he let his body take over. He simply reacted to whatever Tracee threw at him, bending and twisting and striking as the moment called for. Somehow, they'd ended up on the ground, wrestling for domination. Donovan had not wanted to be in this situation—where

Donovan was strong, Tracee made up for it with flexibility. She could twist her body into knots.

Tracee maneuvered her lithe body, snaking her arms and legs around Donovan's like a pretzel, trapping him. Donovan forced her arms apart and turned around so that his full weight was on top of her. They were so close he could smell the sweat that rolled down her chest. It wasn't unpleasant—he felt that familiar tingling in his arms and legs.

He held Tracee down. She struggled to maneuver out of his grip. Suddenly, she stopped and looked at him. Their faces were already mere inches away from each other. Tracee moved infinitesimally forward, her eyes drilling into his with curiosity, a blue steak of her hair plastered to her face.

Donovan moved forward, too. At the last second, he moved his face to the right, never letting his skin make contact with hers, then whispered in her ear, "I win."

The wait continued. Donovan kept a physical distance from Tracee after their last encounter in the gym, but otherwise acted completely normally. He had to admit to himself that he had been sorely tempted to kiss her, and he couldn't let that happen again. He didn't want to give her any ideas either. Donovan had to think of his wife, his kids. They were the reason he was there in the first place.

Finally, after a long week of waiting and very little sleep, Colonel McGregor stormed into one of their gatherings.

"I've been looking for you guys everywhere!" he shouted. "How do expect anyone to deliver news at the first signs of progress if you hide away in a supply closet?!"

"We were, uh...," Jonathan said.

"Where's everyone's watches?" Colonel McGregor asked. "I've been calling for hours."

They all spluttered for a moment, not wanting to admit that they'd silenced the watches so they could concentrate for a couple of hours. They hadn't suspected that anything would happen this fast.

"We were planning," Tracee said quickly. "You know, a backup plan, in case you guys couldn't figure it out."

"Well, no need for that anymore," Colonel McGregor said. "It's done."

"What?" Donovan asked. "So fast? How did..."

"Do you want to sit here and question me or do you want to *see* it?"

Donovan, Tracee, and Jonathan raced for the door.

Colonel McGregor led them into the partition on the fifty-fourth floor. There was a single table in it and two chairs. On the table were piles and piles of papers covered in drawings. On top of the papers was a small black device.

"How does it work?" Tracee asked.

"You scan a person's brain waves," Captain Umar said, picking up the device and waving it in front of Tracee's face. "Like so. Then you save the data." Captain Umar pushed a button. "Then..." He pushed Tracee out of the door. "...you select the brain waves you want to track and hit the seek button."

Captain Umar pressed another button and the device started to hum in his hand, then it was beeping. He walked slowly up to Tracee. It beeped faster the closer he got. When he was within one foot of her, the device let out one last high pitched beep.

"*Target found,*" it said.

Chapter 10

"Cloning will enable mankind to reach eternal life."
$$-\text{Claude Vorilhon}$$

May 15, 2176
Fort Belvoir, VA
Donovan Knight

They connected the device to the satellites on top of the building. It would give the device an infinitely wider range. They set it up to track any brain waves within a 2% similarity to Tobias's. After another couple of days, it found what it was looking for.

"It was a previously unknown planet," Colonel McGregor was saying to General Umar. "We don't know when Tobias discovered it, but the clone is definitely there. I have no doubt."

"Upon further investigation," Captain Umar said, "we found that the planet is habitable. It's nowhere near as flourishing with life as Earth, but it has water and breathable air.

"In addition, when we looked through the pictures of Tobias's lab we found one of this very planet with its coordinates. The location had been hiding under our noses the whole time. Tobias had placed a label on it. It said 'Planet Lohiri.' He's named it. We have yet to find anything else."

"This is fabulous news," General Umar said. "You guys did great work. Now it's time to get a good night's rest. Tomorrow, you'll travel to this new planet to see if you can uncover more clues."

"Yes, sir." They were dismissed.

Donovan lay in bed that night wide awake, his mind still buzzing from all that had happened that day. It was late before his mind finally calmed down and allowed him to rest.

The next day they set out for Lohiri. They suited up in space force uniforms. Even though tests had shown that the air was breathable, they wore oxygenated helmets just in case.

They arrived on the quiet rocky planet but didn't disembark. They stayed on the ship and observed the land from above, looking for anything interesting.

They used the brain wave tracker to lead them to Tobias's clone. Tracee flew the vessel in the direction indicated by the device. Eventually, they spotted a building. It was odd, being on an alien planet and seeing a structure that could have been built on earth. The landed nearby.

They were surprised when nothing happened. There were no attackers—no Tobias there to confront them.

It was pretty anticlimactic.

"Well, let's get moving. Can't sit here all day," Donovan said.

"But what if it's a trap?" Captain Umar asked.

"Then if we fall into it, we'll run for it. But we have to try and explore at least a little."

Reluctantly, they all left the ship. The weight of the guns and e-guns in their holsters was of some comfort. If Tobias did show up, at least they all had two types of weapons—one of them had to work.

The building was a lot bigger up close. It reached into the purple sky, towering above their heads. There were a set of glass double doors under a three-story archway.

Donovan felt like an ant.

The doors opened when they approached.

Donovan was suspicious. It was just too easy, too inviting. They walked inside. Donovan became even more alert to his surroundings. He heard the footfall of every comrade behind him.

They crept further and further into the lion's den, finding nothing but large, white echoing rooms and chambers, all of them empty.

"This can't be it," Colonel McGregor said. "We can't have come here for an empty building."

They delved deeper and finally came upon metal science equipment stored in the rooms. None of it was in use, but at least it was something other than empty air.

Donovan led them into the largest room yet. It was filled to the brim with stainless steel. There were hundreds of devices, all of them exactly the same, lined up in perfectly neat rows.

They each resembled a dentist's chair. There were large tables and contraptions that hung over them sporting hundreds of tools, most of which had sharp points. Underneath each chair was a storage cabinet.

"What the hell is all this stuff?" Captain Umar asked.

Donovan realized that he recognized the devices. He hadn't really been paying attention at the time, but there was one of these things in the secret room in Tobias's lab back on Earth.

These machines were used for cloning.

With these machines, Tobias could make hundreds of clones at once. Based on his last encounter with a clone, Donovan thought that one was enough. The sight of the lab—designed for the mass production of human clones—chilled Donovan to the bone. It was extremely eerie. The emptiness made it even more so.

They crept around the place, finding nothing but sterile equipment.

Then, from seemingly nowhere, a figure appeared. It was a hologram.

Tracee whipped out her gun in less than a second and fired. The bullet only disrupted the surface of the image, sending pixels scattering for a moment then landing in the far wall.

The hologram smiled.

Donovan looked at it in the eyes. "What is it that you find so amusing, grandfather?"

Tobias raised his eyebrows. "Grandfather? I have no grandchildren that I know of." He chuckled then. "Well, of course. They found the virus then. And of course they would use *my* invention and send my own descendants against me. Fools. Tell me boy, what time are you from?"

"2258." Donovan didn't know what else to do but answer him. Maybe he was just in shock.

"So it took them that long, did it?" Tobias chuckled again. "What do you all want from me?"

"The cure to this crazy virus." Tracee said.

"I can't do that."

"Why not?" Donovan asked.

The hologram sighed. "None of you would understand. You haven't done the things that I've done. Seen the things that I've seen. It would be difficult to explain." Here Tobias took on a mournful look.

"Well, try anyway," Donovan said. He was suddenly very angry. This man wasn't his grandfather. This man who spoke in such a cloying tone. This man didn't even know Donovan. And apparently the future version of Tobias didn't care if Donovan lived or died, either.

Tobias looked at Donovan for a moment as if searching for something in his eyes. Finally, he nodded. "Very well."

He paused, collecting his thoughts. "I grew up learning about the marvels and miracles of science in the slums of West Haven. The human race had saved the planet from destruction by ending global warming, they had brought back extinct species and rebuilt natural habitats, and they cleaned up and eliminated all of the world's trash. It would seem that humans should be living in a utopia. But that was not that case.

"Humans still hoarded resources. Greed, murder, theft— all were rampant, not only in the slums but in the rich cities. In fact, it was the rich who had access to unlimited resources who withheld life-giving materials from the poor. They charged us double for water and food. Living in the slums was a day-to-day fight for survival.

"I've seen men murdered over a loaf of bread. Children beaten and robbed for a single bottle of water. They pitted us against one another, waiting for us to kill each other off. Police were no help. They were all corrupt. They would only help if you had enough money to pay them, and no one did except for drug lords and food smugglers.

"Yes, I've seen awful, terrible things. Things that should never have happened when there was unlimited clean water, power, and food just ten miles away in the next city. I went to school religiously, studied every day so that one day I could escape from that evil place. I learned the sciences and created new things—things that I'd hoped to use to help people in the slums.

"However, whenever I tried to use my inventions to aid the poor, the government stopped me at every turn. There was always some law, some reason why my plans wouldn't work. To think, mere words on paper holed up in some congressional library stopped me from saving real human lives with my advanced technology!

"That's when I began to defy the government. I work with them now, yes, but I have long since stopped working *for* them, like some blind dog sent to its master's bidding. I wouldn't be their slave anymore. I would create justice, whether they liked it or not.

"For a while, that's exactly what I did—I created justice. I fed people. I clothed them. All anonymously, of course. But then a day came where I lost hope in even the victimized people of the slums."

Tobias paused for a moment.

"I was married once, you know." The hologram toyed with a golden band on its finger. A look of longing came across Tobias's face. Then the look turned to anger and disgust.

"My wife, Deidra. Your grandmother, if you're really my grandson. And you must be—you look so like me, so like your father, too. Your grandmother knew about everything I was doing. I had met her in school. She was a biology major. Smart, beautiful, funny. She was a remarkable woman. She was born and raised in a wealthy city, but she visited the slums quite often, giving out food and water to those who needed it. She believed in my cause and she helped me.

"One day, we were touring the slums at night with food. The meals were free and we came to this particular area frequently. There was a boy. About seventeen. We saw him every time we went. He was always very polite, always giving, sharing with his two younger siblings. That day, his little brother and sister weren't with him. When I asked where they were he looked nervous.

"We were beginning to serve the food when he pulled out an e-gun. He aimed it at Deidra. Three other boys, all of them a few years older, came over and pulled out guns too. The young boy commanded us to give him all of the food. I tried to talk him down, to awaken his empathy—there was a line of people, many of them children and elderly. But he wouldn't listen.

"He grew impatient with what he called my 'rambling.' He said he didn't care about everyone else—so long as he survived and found a way to make money, he was happy. The food smugglers had made him a deal. They'd wanted to teach Deidra and me a lesson—we'd been stealing their business by giving away food. So they bribed the boy to rob us.

"For good measure, he shot my wife in the heart. She died instantly, but I had to watch her body writhe on the ground from the electric shocks."

Tobias was caught up in the memory. The hologram was so clear that Donovan could see the tears well up in Tobias's eyes. Donovan almost began to feel sorry for him. Tobias collected himself and continued.

"I never returned to the slums again. Deidra was everything to me. The boy whom we had fed for months, showing him nothing but caring and kindness, killed my wife for a couple thousand dollars.

"When I looked at the world around me, all I could find was corruption. Visits outside the U.S. did nothing to dispel those findings. Genuine kindness was a rarity. Everyone pursued their own ends blindly, never giving thought to anyone else.

"That's when I made my decision."

"What decision?" Donovan asked.

He'd been listening to the story in half amazement, half horror. He knew the things that went on in slums—both Tobias and Nona had grown up in them—but he'd never heard of starvation and murder in the streets. Nona had never mentioned it. Perhaps Tobias's slum had been worse than any of the others. Or perhaps Nona decided to keep that darkness to herself.

"Why did you never tell me about my grandmother? You told me she died in a skycar accident."

"I don't know, dear boy. I haven't withheld that information from you yet, have I?" Tobias suddenly lost the gloomy air with which he'd told his story and chuckled at Donovan's momentary lack of common sense. "But I imagine I will keep all this from you in the hopes of keeping you pure. I've never told any of this to your father, either. I'm hoping that he will be the just and loving ruler over one of my new countries on earth. Maybe the future me saw the same potential in you. It's perfect, really, my own blood taking up the major leadership positions."

They all stared at Tobias in angry shock.

Tracee was the first to react. "*What?* What do you mean, *ruler* of new countries?"

Donovan was about to ask the same thing despite the fact that he had a good idea of what his grandfather would say.

"Oh, hadn't I gotten to that part yet?" Tobias waited dramatically. "The virus is designed to destroy the human race from the inside out. I'm going to kill you all and start over with a new human race—all of whom will be descended from me."

"You're insane." Colonel McGregor spoke for the first time.

Tobias laughed—Colonel McGregor seemed to particularly amuse him. "I thought the same thing once. I said to myself— why Tobias, how can you create a whole human race from your own genes? It would never last—not enough diversity.

"But then I came up with a brilliant idea. Surely, out of all the billions of people on earth, there had to be at least, say, a couple thousand worth saving. I began to look for people. I found a few here and there—people doing kind deeds, not for gain but out of the goodness of their hearts. Those were the people that I would save. Those were the people worthy of breeding with my master race."

This time Jonathan was the first to recover. "This guy must be shitfaced. He can't be serious." He shook his head, looking back and forth between Donovan and the hologram. "He isn't *really* serious right now, is he?"

"I think he is," Tracee said.

Donovan stood, frozen. His mind couldn't fathom it. Flashes of heat ran up and down his body. This man wasn't his grandfather. He couldn't be.

"How could I have not seen this?" Donovan said. "I knew you. You raised me. How could I have not seen this—this madness?"

"I can actually answer that for you," Tobias said. "You see, *I* never really raised you. If what you say is true and you're really from the year 2258, then I will have transferred my consciousness by then."

Donovan stared blankly.

"The clone?" Tobias continued. He spoke as if to someone who was very slow. "The one you found in my lab? I created it as a blank slate. It doesn't have a mind of its own, like the others. Essentially it's just an empty shell. When this body becomes too old, I'll transfer my consciousness into that one. However, this body..." The hologram pointed to himself. "...will retain an imprint of some of my memory and personality. Perhaps the Tobias that raised you went soft. Or maybe, as I said earlier, that version of me found something in you worth saving and decided not to spoil your innocence."

Tobias shrugged. "Maybe he chose not to show you this—ah—'madness,' as you say."

"That's why my grandfather got sick! That's why his mind began to deteriorate. He—he forgot who he was."

"Did he?" Tobias leaned forward. "I was curious what would happen to this body once I left it behind. Thank you for telling me that, dear boy. You have deeply satisfied my curiosity."

That's when it all clicked. This wasn't the man who Donovan had known. This Tobias was wrong—the grandfather he knew didn't see him as a pawn to be used in his plans—didn't see him as a future ruler—he genuinely wanted to protect Donovan from the horrors of the world.

Donovan had not noticed any insanity in his grandfather—except on those rare times, probably when the evil in him took over—because it was never there. Donovan was convinced—when Tobias switched over to his new body he took most of his evil nature with him, leaving the empty body with mostly goodness.

Somehow, even knowing that only an imprint of a human being had raised him, Donovan was immensely relieved. He was able to disconnect the man before him from the man he knew. This person was a stranger. He was insane. It made him sad to think of the wonderful person Tobias had the potential to be.

There's no time for sympathy, Donovan told himself. *It's my job to stop him.*

They had already gotten a good deal of information out of him, but Donovan wanted to keep him talking.

"Your 'master race'—where is it? You have all this cloning equipment but you haven't gotten very far, have you?"

"Oh, I've done wonders. Here, alone on this planet, I've put all my time into replicating myself. I have hundreds of clones here. Just because you haven't found them yet doesn't mean they don't exist. They helped me build this place. They've helped me make a considerable amount of progress with my plans."

"Right," Donovan said. "World domination."

Tobias looked truly affronted. "Domination? No, child, this will be a *cleansing*. The world will be born anew. It will finally become the utopia it should have been two hundred years ago!" Tobias spoke faster, caught up in his passion. "Yes, a utopia... a perfect world filled with perfect people. My descendants will be the best humans to ever walk this earth. They'll be the strongest, the fastest, the most intelligent!"

"A bit full of himself, isn't he?" Jonathan said to Donovan.

Tobias laughed. "This isn't mere wishful thinking, *boy*. I specifically enhanced my clones to have better sight, better hearing, a better sense of smell, more strength, rapid cell regeneration."

"Rapid cell regeneration?" Captain Umar asked. "That's impossible."

"Silly boy, of course it isn't. I created it. I gave them all the features we humans lost when we got our big brains. I've given them their animalistic strengths back—all without losing the cognitive ability of the human brain."

"But that's—it's not...," Captain Umar stuttered.

"Everything is possible! If only you push your mind to its limits and discover how it can be done! I am a genius, child. Or did you forget with whom you are speaking?"

Captain Umar was about to make an angry retort when Tracee spoke. "Wait a minute. If you've been here all this time, making clones as you claim, then the man who's in China is also..."

"A clone, yes. Smart girl."

Everyone spun around. The voice had come not from the hologram but from right behind them. The real life, flesh-and-blood Tobias stood with his arms folded across his chest. He wore a grey suit with a white lab coat on top. He gave them all a friendly smile.

Tracee raised her gun. Everyone else followed her lead.

Donovan stepped forward with his arms spread. "No. Wait." He gestured for them to lower their weapons.

"Donovan," Tracee said, keeping her gun aimed. "We can't let him escape."

"Yes, but if you kill him then we may never get a cure."

"Now that we've found this place we're sure to find it. It has to be around here somewhere."

"We don't even know that there *is* a cure. What if he never created one? We need him. Alive."

"Why thank you, dear boy. I rather appreciate not having my brains blown out all over the floor by that primitive weapon."

"I didn't do it for you," Donovan snapped. "We still have e-guns with non-lethal settings. I won't hesitate to use them on you if your answers are not satisfactory."

Tobias smiled, as if amused by some private joke.

"Tell us. Have you made a cure?"

"Why, as a matter of fact I have," Tobias said. He turned and took a step to the left. Everyone stepped forward, expecting him to make some sudden move to kill them, but he merely began to leisurely pace the floor.

"I have a cure, yes. For those deserving of it."

"And who are you to decide who lives and dies?" Colonel McGregor demanded.

Once again, Tobias seemed to be particularly amused by McGregor.

"My genius," Tobias replied. "My intellect is superior to any human brain that has ever come before. It has pierced the depths of time and space. Even with clear explanations and instructions, there only a rare human who can truly understand the things that I've discovered. I think that puts me in a position to make the wisest choices."

"Enough of this! Where is it?" Jonathan asked. He moved forward and held his e-gun directly in front of Tobias's face.

Tobias didn't flinch even a centimeter. His expression didn't change.

"I can understand your frustration," Tobias said. "You care about people, don't you, boy? You want to save them. You don't want anyone to die. But trust me, it's better this way. You're too young and too privileged to understand."

Jonathan pushed the e-gun closer to Tobias's face.

"Jonathan...," Donovan said in a calming tone. "Relax." A shot at that range, even non-lethal, could have lasting effects. They wanted Tobias's brain to be perfectly unharmed.

"I'm relaxed," Jonathan said. His face didn't turn away from Tobias. "Where is it?"

"I'd like to make you an offer," Tobias said. "All of you. You all seem to be rather good people. You came here, risking you lives on a mission to save the human race from certain death. It's all very noble. You are exactly the type of people the new earth will need. With time, I think you can be convinced that I'm right about the world."

"We'll never join you."

"There are benefits," Tobias said, ignoring Jonathan. He looked at the rest of them in turn, eyes resting on Donovan the longest. "There is much more to the virus than you know. It is only a primer—a blank slate, if you will."

Donovan rolled his eyes. "Fine. I'll bite. What are you talking about?"

"The virus that has infected the planet is merely a primer that is activated to do one thing or another by coming into contact with a formula. The virus that I issued contains a formula that tells it to attack the cells of its host. But the formula has a thick coat—one that only fades away after many years. That's why the virus seemed to be so slow-acting. That's why it appears to be harmless at first. The formula is undetectable unless you already know it's there.

"The other formula, which I offer to you now, once injected into the bloodstream, will prompt the virus to actively protect the cells of its host. It will give you powerful healing abilities. It sharpens your sight, gives you strength— essentially all of the abilities that my clones have.

"If you join me, you will have the formula as a reward. Not a bad bonus, eh?"

"We don't want your stupid formula, Tobias," Captain Umar said. "Who knows what else you've hidden inside it?"

"Are you sure?" Tobias asked, as if they had all turned down a cookie or a refreshing glass of water. "I will not offer it again."

They all stared at him stonily.

"Donovan?" Tobias asked. "Will you not join your grandfather on his righteous quest? I wouldn't be so blind and callous as to exclude your family. They, too, would receive the formula. It would reverse the current effects of the virus. They'd all be healed. Return to your own time. Find me. Join me."

Donovan was torn. He hated this man more with each word that he spoke. He was planning to kill off all humans on the planet... and yet, Donovan was very tempted to take him up on his offer. He could save his family. He could return to the future and be his own self... and not disappear.

He could do it easily. He could eliminate his team right now. They'd never expect it.

Of course, though he wanted desperately for his family to survive, Donovan couldn't kill his comrades. He could never work with Tobias. He would have to find another way.

"Tobias," Donovan said. "Turn yourself in. Come back with us. Reform yourself. If you can't do that, at least just leave earth alone. Start your new race here, on this planet, and leave us be. And if we fall into chaos and murder and treachery, then so be it. Give us the cure and let us figure out the problems on Earth for ourselves. You can have your utopia. Right here."

Tobias sighed deeply. "I had really hoped you would come to my side, boy. You had such great potential."

Donovan thought of the Tobias who raised him—the Tobias with so much good intent for the world. Surely that person had to be somewhere inside this Tobias—after all, he was the original copy.

"Somewhere inside you," Donovan said, "there is a good man. I know because I've met him. He raised me. The Tobias I knew never could have conceived of what you have done. That man is more present in you than you realize—why else would you have told us so much? Why else would you have given away so much detail about your virus and your plans? Is it that, secretly, you want someone to stop you?"

Tobias let out a long, hearty laugh. "I'm not crying out with my soul to be saved, Donovan. You're so naïve. It's almost endearing.

"What you haven't realized is that it doesn't matter what I tell you—I've already won. No matter how much information you gain, no matter how much effort you put into destroying me—my plan is full proof. The world is at stake here—this is chess, not checkers, boy. I already have you at checkmate.

"And now that I see that you will not join me, no matter how great the benefits, there is but one choice left—I must destroy you all!"

Tobias sprang forward, a knife withdrawn in a flash from the inside of his lab coat.

Donovan raised an arm instinctively to block him, but before Tobias could even touch Donovan, he fell to the ground, convulsing.

Tracee had shot him. She quickly clicked a pair of electric cuffs around his wrists. The convulsing slowed but didn't stop.

Before Donovan could thank her for the save, the sounds of rapid footsteps echoed from the hallway. They had no time to prepare—the clones were upon them.

The room filled with them in an instant. Dozens upon dozens of Tobiases everywhere. They had no choice now. Donovan gave the command to shoot to kill.

"Fire at will!" he shouted.

There was an echoing laugh that rolled through the room like an ocean wave. The Tobiases were chortling joyfully.

"You can't kill me," they said. "I'm everywhere."

The words reverberated through the room. *I'm everywhere. I'm everywhere. I'm everywhere.*

Donovan was barely aware of the fight that ensued. The only thought that reared its ugly head inside his mind was that they had yet to find a cure. If they didn't find it now, they might never find it. But they had no time. No way to look for it.

They could barely manage to survive the onslaught of strengthened clones and escape that place, let alone conduct a search for the cure. It was impossible. Donovan felt devastation begin to overwhelm him, but he continued to fight. He had to survive. He couldn't give up.

The clones were immensely more powerful than his team. At first they used their guns, knowing that e-guns would have little to no effect. They managed to take out several dozen clones. They scattered the floor in piles, blood flowing freely over the white tiles.

Tables were upended, equipment destroyed by stray bullets. The bodies piled up, but there seemed to be no end to them.

Then, to Donovan's horror, the clones that had received seemingly fatal shots to the heart or major arteries rose from the floor like zombies, skin flowing back together as if God's hand had lain across the wounds, melting the clay back smooth.

For the first time in his life, Donovan didn't know what to do but run.

"Aim for the head!" he shouted. "Run whenever you can. Head for the ship. We have to get out of here *now*!"

He wasn't positive that they'd all heard him. He didn't even have time to look around and see if they were all still alive. He saw Tracee still fighting out of the corner of his eye.

Donovan pulled the trigger on his gun as fast as he could, shooting foreheads left and right with perfect accuracy. A path began to clear in front of him. He kept shooting.

Tracee came up behind him and added her bullets. They started falling quickly, clearing a way.

"Over here!" Tracee said.

Donovan heard the others run up behind him. He chanced a glance. Everyone was still there. A cut above Jonathan's eyebrow was bleeding into his face. His limped a little—his leg sporting a mass of blood from some wound.

Captain Umar's arm was limp at his side. His face was white as milk, but he bravely used the other arm to continue shooting. Colonel McGregor seemed to be okay.

"Umar, McGregor, take the left. Tracee, Jonathan, take the right. I'll lead. Whatever you do, don't let them touch you!"

Donovan made every effort not to let the clones touch him. He knew that if they got hold of him it might all be over. They could fatally injure him with a punch to the right place. At the thought of this, an image of Eric swam in his head— eyes bulging, spit flying from his mouth as the clone in the lab punched him in the stomach.

Donovan couldn't let them land a single blow. He kept shooting. Soon, he needed to reload.

"I'm out!"

"Switch with me," Tracee said. She stepped in front of him and kept firing.

Donovan took her place beside Jonathan. Jonathan covered him while he reloaded his gun. When he was finished, he switched with Tracee again.

In this way they shifted as needed and forged a bloody walkway through the sea of clones. Donovan wasn't aware of when it happened, but finally they broke through.

Suddenly, there were hundreds of clones behind them and none in front of them.

They ran.

Jonathan quickly fell behind. Looking back, Donovan could tell that he was in severe pain trying to keep up the pace. But if they slowed down even a little, the clones would catch them. They were fast.

At frequent intervals, Donovan slowed down until he was in the back of the group, leaving Tracee to lead. Then he ran backwards and shot the closest clones, covering Jonathan so that he could catch up.

They turned corners and burst through doors, trying to get to the exit.

At some point Donovan realized that Jonathan wasn't going to make it. He gave Jonathan his gun as they ran and, without stopping, swung the boy over his shoulder.

"Shoot them!" he shouted.

Donovan heard the fire of the weapons resounding in his ears. He heard satisfying thuds as clones fell to the ground.

When they approached the main door, a heart-sinking thought occurred to Donovan—what if they had destroyed the ship?

They burst through the doors.

To Donovan's relief, the ship was still there. They ran to it. Some of them stumbling over rocks. The clones still pursued them. Donovan wondered if they would follow the team to earth.

Tracee opened the ship doors as they approached and they all ran safely inside. Tracee hurriedly hit the button to close the door. The clones were almost to the ship.

The door crept closed.

Too slowly.

Before it could swing shut, the first clone reached it and wrenched it back open. Tracee kicked it hard in the stomach. Donovan doubt that it was hurt, but it lost its balance and fell to the ground below.

"Tracee! Fly the ship. We'll take care of the clones."

Tracee did as Donovan said while the rest of them kept firing outside the door, trying not to let another one get that close. Donovan pulled a second gun from his holster.

The engines flared. The ship began to rise slowly from the ground. Donovan ran out of ammo. A few seconds later, so did Jonathan. Captain Umar was sitting down, clutching his arm, unable to hold off the pain and fight.

Colonel McGregor kept up his fire. But it was hardly enough to keep all of them back.

The ship was three feet off the ground when a wall of clones reached the half-open door. Donovan pushed McGregor back and tried to close it, but the nearest clone pushed its arm in and pulled it open.

Donovan mimicked what Tracee had done earlier and kicked it full in the stomach. But the force of bodies behind the clone steadied it. It was able to maintain its grip. The ship rose another five feet from the ground, leaving the rest of the clones to glare up at them, frustration and hate in their eyes.

The one Tobias who had made it onto the ship leapt at Donovan, fist raised. Donovan ducked underneath its arms to the open door.

General McGregor aimed his gun and fired, but his gun clicked impotently—he had run out of bullets.

The clone pushed McGregor roughly to the side. He banged his head on the metal wall of the cabin and lay on the floor, unconscious.

The clone charged Donovan again, the light of victory shining on its face.

At the last second, Donovan dodged to the left.

The clone tried to pull up short, to grab onto something, but its momentum carried it away. It flew through the door and landed on the ground twenty feet below. Donovan looked down at its crumpled body and did not feel triumph.

He was exhausted and half his team was injured. They had made it out alive. The natural extinct of his body was to feel relief.

But his heart and mind knew the truth—they had survived this fight—but Tobias would win.

They hadn't found a cure.

Tracee opened up a teleportation field and flew through it. They traveled through the wormhole toward home, toward Earth.

They had survived, but they were already dead.

Chapter 11

"Victorious warriors win first and then go to war, while defeated warriors go to war first and then seek to win."

—Sun Tzu

May 16, 2176
Fort Belvoir, VA
Donovan Knight

Donovan and the others arrived at Fort Belvoir in silence.

Donovan instructed the others to get medical assistance while he and Tracee reported to General Umar. He commanded them to search Tobias's lab in Atlanta one more time, just in case they missed something. Maybe there was another hidden door they hadn't found.

Donovan thought it was pointless but did it anyway—despite the aches in his body from fighting Tobias's clones—just so he could feel like he was doing *something*. Colonel McGregor had suffered a pretty hard hit on the head—he was still out cold. Jonathan and Captain Umar were having their shattered limbs repaired piece by piece.

Donovan and Tracee conducted the search. They returned to Tobias's house. They looked everywhere. To Donovan's surprise, they found a hidden safe under a single tile in the floor of the secret room.

Inside it was a single vial, about the length of a drinking straw. Donovan was sure he knew exactly what was inside. Tobias had put it there on purpose. They were supposed to find it. What Tobias wanted them to do with it, Donovan didn't know. More than likely, it was a trap.

When they showed it to General Umar, he had it sent to Captain Umar's team for testing.

"Rest while you can," he said. "I'll be summoning you again as soon as the results are in. It shouldn't take too long."

Donovan retreated to his room. Too exhausted to shower, he fell on top of the sheets and fell asleep immediately.

The summons came a few hours later. Donovan stretched the weariness from his limbs and reported to General Umar's office. Tracee and Captain Umar were there. Captain Umar's arm was in a sling. He still looked a little pale but, on the whole, much improved.

"We have the results," he said. "The vial contains the strengthening formula that Tobias told us about. We estimate that it's enough for a dozen people. The question is—what do we do with it?"

"Are you sure that's all that's in there? There's nothing hidden in it?"

"I looked at it myself," Captain Umar said. "As far as I can tell, it's just formula. I could be wrong of course, but..."

General Umar waved a hand. "Oh, stop being modest. You're the brightest mind in biology. If you say that's all there is, then that's all there is."

Captain Umar blushed and looked down. "Thank you, Father."

It was the first time Donovan had heard Captain Umar acknowledge that General Umar was his father.

The General nodded.

"So," Donovan said. "The question is what do we do next?"

"Well, isn't it obvious?" General Umar said. "We must prepare ourselves for battle."

"Battle?" Donovan said, alarmed. "We can't go into battle with Tobias! Those clones would crush us."

"As long as we have the proper weapons, we'll be fine."

"You weren't there. You didn't have to fight them off. They heal just as quickly as you can shoot them down. They're *strong*. If they get their hands on you, you're dead. They can jump higher, move faster, see farther... it's too dangerous. It should be a last resort."

"This *is* the last resort, Donovan. What would you have us do? Conduct more searches? There is nowhere left to search. Judging by the last two attempts, I don't think that's a good idea anyway."

"I'm just saying that we shouldn't rush into it," Donovan argued. "Give me some time to think. I'll come up with something."

"We don't have time," General Umar said. "Tobias could strike at any moment. We must catch him off guard."

"And the formula?" Donovan asked. "You don't plan to use it, do you?"

"Of course not." Something about the way the General's eyes shifted made Donovan suspicious.

"Then what will you do with it?"

"I'm going to let the T.M.A.C.P.U. deal with it. I'm going to call a meeting and get everyone's input. It's not for me to decide what to do with such a thing. I can't decide who lives and dies. I can't decide who to give that power to."

Donovan accepted his answer tentatively.

"But wait," Tracee interrupted.

Donovan had almost forgotten she was there.

"Shouldn't we be using this to our advantage? Shouldn't we use the formula on our best soldiers and give ourselves a fighting chance?"

General Umar looked at her speculatively.

"No—I don't trust it," Donovan said. "We can't trust anything having to do with Tobias."

"He's right," General Umar said. "We can't use it. We must hand it over to the T.M.A.C.P.U."

"Thank you, General," Donovan said. "But please reconsider giving me more time to think. I know Tobias is up to something. What if—what if this whole thing is only a distraction? What if the cure is closer to us than we think? Hidden in plain sight?"

Both Umars looked skeptical.

"Just think about it," Donovan said, beginning to pace with his frenzied thoughts. "Tobias is a master of deception— we know this. The facilities on Lohiri look like a fortress, look like a place where something important would be hidden and defended. But what if that was all a façade? I mean, we got in there easily enough. What if he just wants to draw our attention to Lohiri so that we don't look at other places?"

"I'm sorry, Donovan," General Umar said. "That's a good hypothesis, but there's no real evidence to support that. What we do know for sure is that Tobias has an army on Lohiri—and we cannot allow that army to exist. It is a threat that must be eliminated."

"You're sentencing your men to death."

"They will have everything they need to have a fair shot."

Donovan shook his head stubbornly. "They'll all die."

"I'm sorry that you think that way. We will attack in 48 hours. You will lead the soldiers against Tobias's clones."

A stone fell onto Donovan's chest. He couldn't do it. He wouldn't.

"Yes, sir."

Donovan left the room in a flurry of action. He made an effort not to slam the door behind him. He returned to his room, sickened by the discussion. His whole team would be sent into battle. Tracee, Jonathan, Captain Umar, Colonel McGregor—they would all die.

This was their duty, wasn't it? This is what they'd signed up for. They were prepared to risk their lives.

Not like this!

We can't die like this.

He had to think of something.

Someone knocked on the door. It was Tracee.

She rushed inside and stood in the middle of the room, breathing hard.

"Tracee," Donovan said, seeing the look on her face. "What is it?"

She crossed the room in one stride and threw herself onto him. Her mouth met his with the force of a passionate attack. For a moment, caught up in the hopeless emotion of knowing that he would die soon, he kissed her back.

The warmth of her felt good against him. He pulled her body closer, crushing her. She moaned.

Then, he found his senses. He couldn't do this. Hands trembling, he gently disentangled himself from her embrace.

"I can't do this," Donovan said. "I'm married. I can't"

Tracee held his face in one hand. She looked at him endearingly. "It's 2176," she said. "You're not married yet. Technically..."

"It doesn't matter," Donovan said. "I still remember it. I still love my wife. I can't do this to her."

Tracee looked hurt. She pulled away from him, face contorted with it.

"Fine." She slowed her breathing. "I'll just... go."

Donovan sat on the bed and nodded. He couldn't look at her. He heard the door close.

He took a deep breath and let it out slowly. He couldn't believe he'd let that happen. He'd flirted with her too much. Led her to believe that something between them was possible.

He would apologize later. Right then, he had to think. He had to find a way out of this. He began to pace the floor.

Nothing of any brilliance came to him. As he made his away across the room for what seemed the hundredth time, a clicking noise came from his computer.

Donovan looked at it. The machine had turned on of its own accord.

Donovan stared, frowning, as the screen lit up. An image came into focus.

It was a live feed.

The video showed a large room. In it were General Umar, Captain Umar, Colonel McGregor—when had *he* woken up and why wasn't Donovan told?—Jonathan, and Tracee. What the hell was going on? Why were they meeting without him?

Donovan walked over to the screen. He sat in the desk chair without moving his eyes. He recognized that room—it was the high security vault of floor fifty-eight. Why were they gathered there of all places? And, more importantly, where was this feed coming from? Why was he seeing this?

It couldn't be some coincidental wiring mishap. Someone wanted him to see this, but who?

Before Donovan could think too deeply on it, the voice of General Umar came through the speaker, loud and clear. Donovan jumped in his seat, startled.

"We will attack the day after tomorrow," General McGregor said. "It is doubtful that Brigadier General Knight will cooperate. If that is the case, Tracee will lead you. You will take the formula to Lohiri. Brigadier General Knight is to know nothing of this. His judgement is too clouded. He will only cause trouble if he finds out.

"Captain Umar, you are to administer the formula to Tracee upon your arrival. The rest of you will do your utmost to protect her. She will be our best shot at killing Tobias. You're sure that your device will work, Captain Umar? Colonel McGregor?"

"Yes, sir," Colonel McGregor said. "I took it with me to Lohiri, just to test a theory I had. All of the clones have slightly different brain waves. Despite being genetic replicas of Tobias, they have minds of their own. I couldn't use it then because we were overwhelmed, but with more soldiers and Tracee's additional strength, I think we should have a shot at finding him. The original was definitely there."

"Good." General Umar addressed them all. "Your mission is to kill Tobias at all costs. We need to make sure that he's dead. Then we can search for a cure unencumbered. If we can't find it, we will rely on Captain Umar's team to create one. It may take time, but the gene won't activate for many years. Our most immediate threat right now is Tobias and his army. Is this understood?"

"I don't think we should do this father," Captain Umar said. "We shouldn't use this formula. I agree with Donovan— we can't trust it. We should give Donovan a little time—just a day or two—to think of a better plan."

Jonathan looked at General Umar hopefully. "I agree with Captain Umar," he said.

General Umar's face froze. "This mission has already been decided. You will either obey or suffer the consequences of insubordination."

He left the room leaving Donovan's team to stew in silence.

The sound of the feed cut off leaving only the silent images of Jonathan talking to Captain Umar. Then, the picture shifted. Another image appeared.

It was Tobias. He was being filmed from the waist up.

"What did I tell you, m'boy?" he said with a sympathetic smile. "Full of lies and deception, your precious world. They have betrayed you. I was right about humans—they're lost. Nothing can bring them back to the light.

"I offer you one last chance, Donovan. Join me. If you agree, come to Lohiri before General Umar attacks. I will handle the problem here and send you back to your own time."

He leaned forward as if to turn off the camera then stopped.

"Oh, before I go—if you chose to come—steal the formula and use it. I left it there for you."

The screen went black.

Donovan's mind was reeling. This was all happening too quickly. He forced his mind to slow down.

Think, Knight. Think hard.

He had to stop them from attacking. Tobias was confident that he would defeat them—and with reason. His army was strong. The Army and Space Force wouldn't be able to win with the amount of soldiers they had at Fort Belvoir now— about a thousand—even if Tracee did take the formula.

They would need ten times as many fighters—that would mean going public with the mission, recruiting soldiers for war. Even if that were possible, Tobias could easily strike before they got organized.

The only reason that General Umar believed he could win was because he had the formula. Donovan was sure that General Umar never meant to attack without it. Maybe Donovan could force him to come up with something else...

That was it!

Donovan knew what he had to do.

He went to Captain Umar's room as quickly as he could without attracting attention. He wanted to run but forced himself not to.

He knocked on the Captain's door, sweat beginning to bead on his forehead from nervous anticipation.

Captain Umar had hardly cracked the door when Donovan pushed his way inside.

"What's going on Knight?" He rubbed his eyes.

"Sorry to wake you, I need to speak with you, it's urgent." The words all tumbled out of his mouth without pauses in between.

"What is it?" He looked a little more alert now.

"This formula that we found," Donovan said. "Are you *absolutely* sure that there's nothing more to it than strengthening?"

Captain Umar nodded slowly. "Yes... I'm sure. Wh...?"

"It wouldn't have any fatal or harmful side effects?"

"I'm pretty sure there's nothing wrong with it. Donovan why are you...?"

"Thanks, Captain," Donovan said. "Gotta go."

Donovan rushed from the room, careful to keep his pace to only a brisk walk.

Next he went to Colonel McGregor's room. He knocked, but no one answered.

Where could he be?

Donovan decided to check the cafeteria first. He got lucky. Colonel McGregor was in line. "Colonel McGregor, could I have a word please?"

Surprised, McGregor stepped out of line.

"What is it?"

"I want to get away from the base for a little while. Care to join me for a bite?"

"Well, I was just about to..."

"Aren't you tired of eating the same things all the time? Let's go out and get something to eat." Donovan looked at him pointedly.

Colonel McGregor raised his eyebrows, understanding lighting up his eyes. "Why, yes, of course. Let's go."

He may not have known what Donovan wanted but he was curious enough to want to find out.

They left the base in a standard army skycar. Once they were outside the base General McGregor started talking, but Donovan just shook his head.

Not yet.

They landed at the edge of a small city about five miles away. They left the sky car and Donovan led Colonel McGregor to a burger stand.

"BG Knight, what's going on?"

"Nothing at all. I'm fine. Order something."

They both ordered food. They waited for it in silence. When they finished eating, Donovan led Colonel McGregor away from the skycar, into the forest.

"Do you have a watch with you?" Donovan asked.

"Yes," McGregor said.

"Let me see it."

McGregor unstrapped his watch and handed it over. Donovan broke it in half and threw it with all his strength. Donovan had left his own watch at the fort.

"What the hell?!" McGregor stuttered. "What on earth is wrong with you?"

Donovan grabbed his arm and led McGregor deeper into the trees. "*Shhh.*"

Colonel McGregor let himself be dragged into a dense part of the forest. When Donovan let go, he shouted, "What the *hell* is going on here?"

"We've been bugged," Donovan said. "I can't explain how I know right now—I have to hurry, but Tobias has the whole base bugged. He's been aware of our every move this whole time."

McGregor's mouth fell open then snapped shut again. "But how...?"

"It doesn't matter. Listen, would it be possible for you to make a tiny microphone that can record what I'm saying without being detected by Tobias's security system on Lohiri?"

"Yes, I think so—but why? You have to tell me something. I'm sure General Umar isn't aware of this little meeting. If you want me to disobey him, you'd better give me a damn good reason."

"I don't have time!" Donovan dragged his hands over his head. He breathed deeply. "Okay. The base is bugged. I can't tell anyone I know without alerting Tobias. I can't bring everyone off the base without arousing suspicion. General Umar would never agree anyway.

"Tobias offered me one last deal. He still wants me to join him. This is my chance to get close to him. I have a better chance at killing him that an army ever would. I need to steal the strengthening formula and meet him.

"But first, I want to try and get the location of the cure from him. That's why I need the recorder. I need it to send what it records directly back to you—just in case he kills me before I can kill him. You're the only person who can make it for me. I can't tell anyone else for fear of letting Tobias know that I'm not going to be joining him. If I stay silent, he'll assume that I'm still thinking it over."

Colonel McGregor finally acquiesced.

"Can you make it in the next twenty-four hours and meet me again for lunch to give it to me?"

"Yes. It's a simple enough device."

Donovan leaned into his face. "Can I trust you with this?"

Colonel McGregor backed away. "Of course you can. I happen to agree that you have a better shot. None of us agrees with General Umar's plan—well, except Tracee."

Donovan flinched at the sound of her name.

"Okay," Donovan said. "Let's go back. Act like nothing important has happened at all. Go to the cafeteria tomorrow at

1600 hours. I'll come in about ten minutes later. Don't order. Act like you're still deciding what to get. I'll invite you to the same burger place."

"Okay. Got it."

"And remember. No watches."

Donovan felt relief sink in on the flight back. He had a plan. It would work. He just needed to have a little patience.

Chapter 12

"I recognize in thieves, traitors and murderers, in the ruthless and the cunning, a deep beauty—a sunken beauty."

—Jean Genet

May 17, 2176
Fort Belvoir, VA
Donovan Knight

The next day Donovan met McGregor in the cafeteria, but McGregor insisted that they eat at the fort. Donovan slammed his plate down at the table and scarfed his food down, wondering why McGregor didn't want to meet him but unable to ask him why. Was he going to betray him? Did he decide not to help Donovan after all?

Donovan saw Tracee watching him from the next table, but he ignored her.

"Hey," Colonel McGregor said when they were finished, "I just remembered. I left my watch in your room. Can I come and get it?"

Suddenly, Donovan understood that Colonel McGregor was up to something.

"Yeah, sure," he said.

They met in his room and Colonel McGregor pulled a small black device, rectangular in shape, out of his jacket pocket. He flipped a switch on the side.

"There," he said. "Now we can talk comfortably."

Donovan looked at him questioningly.

"Oh, it's a signal blocker and signal creator," Colonel McGregor said. "It'll block Tobias's spying system within a ten foot radius. It'll also send out fake signals to his system so that he doesn't see any blind spots. He can't hear us now."

Donovan was instantly euphoric. "You're a genius!"

McGregor shrugged. "I thought that'd be better than having to meet up in the middle of nowhere." He dug into another pocket and withdrew another device, this one like a tiny bead that rolled between his fingers.

"Here's the microphone." He handed it over. "It's already recording and sending the audio to my computer."

"Perfect," Donovan said. He was impressed. Hesekiel McGregor really was the smartest mind in technology. Donovan put the tiny dot into his pocket.

"I need to ask for your help with one last thing," Donovan said. "I need you to hack the fort's security system and open the high security vault that houses the formula."

Colonel McGregor frowned. "How did you know about that?"

"Tobias. He showed me the footage on my computer screen. That's when he made the last offer for me to join him."

"I see."

"Can you do it? Can you open the vault so that the alarm doesn't go off?"

Colonel McGregor nodded. "Of course. I'm a genius, remember?"

For what seemed like the first time in weeks, Donovan laughed.

When the lights went out and the majority of people had gone to bed, Donovan crept along the dim halls to the high security vault. He approached the corner and paused before turning. He'd heard whispers. He chanced a quick peek.

There were soldiers guarding the door to the vault. Four of them. That should be easy enough. They didn't seem to be too alert. They were talking in low voices about what they would do when the graveyard shift was over.

Donovan rounded the corner at full speed, shooting non-lethal bolts as he went. They all hit home before the soldiers even realized what was happening. They collapsed, e-guns clattering on the ground as they slipped from their fingers.

Donovan moved quickly. It was only a matter of time before the shocks wore off. Donovan had set his e-gun to the lowest level—it would only last about five minutes.

He stepped to the door and waited. It was Colonel McGregor's turn now. It seemed like a long time, but only two minutes passed before the door slid to the side, revealing another door with a small screen set in its surface.

Donovan tapped the screen and it lit up revealing a keyboard. He entered the code Colonel McGregor had given him. The door swung open.

A blast of cold air washed over Donovan. The vault was freezing cold. Donovan stepped inside and went straight for drawer 695, where McGregor had told him the formula was stored.

Sure enough, there is was. A test tube filled with what looked like water.

Donovan closed the drawer and turned to leave when a group of soldiers rounded the corner. They paused for a moment, uncomprehending.

Donovan was shocked, too. McGregor had blocked the camera system so that it couldn't see him. So what were these soldiers doing here?

There must have been a shift switch that they hadn't known about.

Donovan jumped into action. There was no chance of convincing them that he was supposed to have the formula—not with the other four soldiers slowly recovering from his volts and rising unsteadily to their feet.

Donovan fired a round of shots, all of which hit the newcomers square in their chests.

Donovan stepped over their bodies and turned the corner, only to bump into a fifth solider who was speaking into the headset that looped around his ear.

All Donovan heard was the word "intruder." Without really thinking, he punched the man in the face. The soldier's head snapped backward and he reeled from the force of the blow. Donovan struck again, breaking his arm. He ripped the headset from his ear and threw it to the ground. He stomped on it until it was in tiny little pieces.

Then he ran.

There would be more soldiers. It would be Donovan against the whole fort. He ran to the nearest medical room that he knew of and locked himself inside. He found a syringe, removed the cap from the test tube, and sucked the formula into it.

He discarded the test tube.

He paused. He hated needles.

He steeled himself, raised his arm, and plunged the needle into this leg, pushing the plunger down.

An odd sensation spread through his limbs—a tingling.

Within seconds, his sore muscles were no longer sore and the tiredness due to the late hour disappeared. With a new confidence, Donovan exited the room.

He strolled down the hallway feeling sort of drunk. For no apparent reason he was really happy. He walked to the elevator at a leisurely pace. He pushed the down button and waited for the elevator that would take him to the basement.

Once there he would steal a space ship and teleport to Lohiri.

The elevator doors slid open, but Donovan didn't go inside. There wasn't enough room—it was packed with soldiers. They streamed out and attacked.

Donovan swung his fists left and right, feeling an extra surge of energy that he just had to release. They all carried bulletproof and electricityproof shields. Donovan punched straight through them.

Then he remembered that he was much stronger now. It was good thing they had the shields or Donovan may have killed them. He resolved to hold back to prevent serious injury. Nevertheless he still broke a few arms by accident.

"Move out of the way!" A voice came from the left.

The soldiers moved away from Donovan to allow General Umar to get through.

"Knight!" he shouted. "What the hell are you doing? Why are you doing this?"

"I saw you," Donovan said. "I saw the meeting you had in the vault. I heard what you were planning to do. You lied to me—betrayed me. My grandfather was right. I'm better off on his side."

General Umar's face turned bright red. Whether from embarrassment at being found out or anger, Donovan didn't know.

Donovan backed into the elevator and pushed the button for the basement. A few soldiers moved to stop him but General Umar commanded them to stop.

"He's used the formula. He's too strong. Let him go."

The doors closed and Donovan was enveloped in silence.

He stole the smallest and fastest space ship and left Fort Belvoir. He turned on the teleporter and zoomed through the wormhole.

Chapter 13

> "There's none so blind as those who will not listen."
> —Neil Gaiman, *American Gods*

May 18, 2176
Fort Belvoir
Captain Brian Umar

Brian Umar was asleep when his father summoned him to his office. He hurriedly got dressed.

He knew what had happened before he even got there. The news had spread like wildfire through the fort. There was far much more activity than usual. Soldiers ran back and forth down the halls. Brian heard them talking about it as they passed him.

Donovan had broken into the high security vault and stolen the formula.

Brian couldn't feel shocked. So many unbelievable, crazy things had happened in the last few days that he hardly believed that he could ever be shocked again. He only wondered why Donovan would do such a thing.

Was he really that stubborn? Did he steal it so that he could go and fight Tobias on his own and prevent the battle from happening? Was he really that noble? Brian wasn't sure, but he didn't believe anything his father said about Donovan being a traitor.

Jonathan, Natalee, and McGregor were gathered in his father's office and they were all discussing why Donovan would react the way he had. Had they really misjudged him so?

"It doesn't matter that we trusted him," the General said. "He's our enemy now. When we attack Lohiri, we will aim to kill him as well as Tobias."

McGregor nodded, quickly accepting the plan.

Natalee and Jonathan looked shocked.

"Do we really need to kill him?" Jonathan asked. "Couldn't we capture him alive? I mean, maybe this is all some kind of misunderstanding. Maybe he's just trying to—I don't know—prevent a battle from taking place. He was against it from the beginning."

Brian was surprised that Jonathan had the same exact idea as him.

"I doubt he's that noble," McGregor said. "He comes from a line of insanity. He probably really did join Tobias."

"This can't be real," Natalee said. "This isn't like him."

"And you know that after only knowing this man for a week?" McGregor said harshly.

She was about to say something angrily when the General spoke.

"That's enough. It doesn't matter. For whatever reason, Knight has betrayed us. We must treat him as we would any other enemy. And that means going for the kill. Is that understood?"

There was a reluctant round of "yes, sirs."

Brian left the meeting thinking deeply. He thought his father overestimated the power his authority had over human emotions. The only one in that meeting who seemed likely to take a lethal shot at Knight was McGregor.

Jonathan clearly admired Knight and saw him as a friend more than a General. And Natalee seemed to have some emotional ties to him. Brian wondered what had gone on between them in the short time that they'd known each other.

In any case, Brian just couldn't convince himself that Donovan had betrayed them. He couldn't explain Donovan's actions in a way that made sense, but he had a good instinct about people. Donovan was still on their side. He just had to prove it somehow.

He went to Jonathan's room and told him his plan. He didn't know if it would accomplish anything, but Jonathan was more than happy to help.

They broke into Knight's room and searched it for clues.

It didn't take long for them to find the cameras.

Jonathan sat heavily in the desk chair. "How come no one has ever found these? They weren't even that well hidden. There's a whole spying system in here. And this cord..."

Jonathan held up a black cable.

"...leads outside this room. The whole place could be bugged. Who knows who's listening to us right now?"

"Maybe no one found it because no one was ever looking for it," Brian said. "I wonder if this is a military spy system—or something else."

They looked at each other.

Jonathan's face mirrored what Brian felt—eerie.

"Let's get out of here," Brian said.

They returned the room to exactly how it'd been before and rushed out the door.

Suddenly, a hand was on Brian's chest, pushing him back inside. The door shut behind them. It was McGregor.

"Were you following us?" Brian asked.

"Yes," McGregor said.

He reached into his pocket and pulled out a small black device. He flipped a switch on its side.

"What is that?" Jonathan asked.

"A signal blocker," McGregor said. "It blocks the spying system. No one can hear us now."

"Wait, how'd you know about the spying system?" Jonathan asked.

"Donovan told me about it," McGregor said. "He's not a traitor."

Well, that was the last thing Brian had expected. "You're a good actor. You seemed ready to have Knight's head back there."

"Well, I had to act natural, didn't I?" McGregor said. "Now, we have to do this quickly. I need your help."

Brian was stunned at the story McGregor told. Tobias had been spying on them all this time. Donovan had found out about it but kept silent to protect them all.

"The spy system actually belongs to the military. I did some research—classified files. It was part of an initiative that Tobias launched years ago for so called security purposes. He's been hacking the military for a long time. Watching our every move."

"We have to tell the General," Brian said.

"I did," McGregor said. "He didn't believe me. He thought that Donovan was making it up to keep him from attacking Tobias. He refused to even conduct a search."

"The fool!" Brian shouted, unable to stop himself. "He's an absolutely stubborn *prick*! He put us all in danger for the sake of his pride! I swear to God, if that man wasn't my father I'd strangle him."

"Calm down, Captain," McGregor said. "Now that you two have actually found the system and can vouch for Donovan, too, maybe he'll listen."

Brain mumbled under his breath, "Idiot old man."

He yanked the door open and they followed him out.

When they reached the General's office, Natalee was already there.

"Can we have a word with you, General?" McGregor said.

Brian let him take the lead.

The General looked at Natalee. "Are we done here?"

"Yes, sir," she said bitterly.

"Wait," Brian said. "She should stay. She'd want to know about this."

Natalee looked back and forth between Brian and McGregor. "What is it? What's going on? Is it Knight?"

Jonathan shut the door.

"Yes," Brian said. "We've found something."

"Out with it, boy! What is it?"

"The same exact thing that McGregor tried to tell you before," Brian said, unable to keep the anger out of his voice. "Donovan is still on our side. Chaplain and I found a spying system in his room. The direction of the cords suggests that it stretches outside his room—it covers the entire base."

The General looked flabbergasted. "But—it can't be—Knight was just saying that to..."

"Look, you old stubborn fool!" Brian shouted, leaning across his father's desk. "Listen to us or we're lost."

The General stared at him in shock but didn't say anything more.

"The system," Brian continued, "was installed as a part of an initiative that Tobias created years ago. He's been spying on us the whole time. He's always known our every move before we ever made it. He's been toying with us. He knows we can't stop him."

"Our only hope is Knight," McGregor said. He pulled the signal blocker from his jacket and quickly explained its purpose. "His mission is protected so long as we keep it to ourselves. We must go on like everything is the same—as if we believe Donovan is a traitor."

"But," Jonathan said, "surely we must do something else? We should look for the cure here on earth, like Donovan said. Maybe he was right and this was all just a distraction. Tobias doesn't want us to find the cure so he's trying to get us to believe that he has it with him, when really it's hidden close to home."

"We can't..." General Umar stopped and cleared his throat, as if the shock of his son's rant had dried it out. "...We can't carry out that massive of an operation without the rest of the base knowing what's going on."

"I'll create a way to send everyone electronic messages that Tobias can't see."

"Good." The General began to gather control again. "Notify me when the message is sent. I will delay the attack by a couple of hours, but that's all I can do without arousing suspicion. After that, we'll proceed as planned—well, at least on the surface. Let the soldiers know that they must not shoot Knight to kill—only to stun and capture. If at all possible, try to miss him altogether so that he can complete his mission. We must all protect his cover.

"I also need you to put together a couple of teams to search all known buildings that were of importance to Tobias."

"Yes, sir," McGregor said. He left the room.

"Sir," Natalee said. "I want to go to Lohiri. I want to be a part of the attacking battalion."

The General stared at her.

"Me, too," Jonathan said. "I want to help Donovan. If his cover is blown and he needs backup, I want to be there."

"That fond of him are you?" the General said, an amused smile playing at his lips. "Go ahead. Serve me where you will."

"Thank you, sir," Natalee said.

"I wish I could be so noble," Brian said, "but I'm afraid I'm not a very good fighter. I'll stay and help out here."

"All right, soldiers, prepare for your parts," the General said. "Get as must rest as you can in the next few hours. I'll summon you when it's time."

Natalee and Jonathan left the room.

"You did a good job there, Father," Brian said. "For a moment I thought your stubbornness would be the end of us."

His father smiled. "I have learned that being right isn't always the best thing. Your mother taught me that. I just wished I had learned it before the divorce."

"Father..." Brian had never heard him speak of the divorce before. He had always avoided the topic.

The General waved his hand as if to wave Brian's words away. "Get on, boy, and help with the efforts. Either get some rest or help Colonel McGregor."

"And what about you, General?" Brian said. "Will you ever rest?"

"Not for a while yet. It's not a General's job to rest."

Brian smiled, feeling for the first time that he really understood his father.

Chapter 14

"You usually have to wait for that which is worth waiting for."

—Carl Bruce

May 20, 2176
Fort Belvoir
Captain Brian Umar

The search parties came up empty. It was a major blow to Brian—he'd had high hopes that they would find something in Tobias's high school science lab where he had discovered Lohiri.

Shortly after the search teams returned to the base, they received news that Tobias's clones had destroyed Natalee's entire stealth unit. From the sound of it there were no survivors. Brian's heart was heavy. He didn't know Natalee that well, but she had been a good soldier—an expert fighter. If the clones had defeated her, he hated to think what would happen to the rest of them.

Just the thought of running into a clone again made Brian shiver. Though his arm had healed by then, he remembered the pain all too vividly. He was in a soldier's uniform, but he certainly didn't feel like a fighter. He was a scientist before anything. He used brain over brawn.

Their only hope was that Knight would discover the location of the cure.

Brian regretted that McGregor had not thought of a way to send Knight a message. He would have liked Knight to know that they didn't think he was a traitor. But he understood that such devices and transmissions were extremely risky.

Knight would have to go it alone. And the rest of them just had to wait until he turned on his microphone.

Chapter 15

"When you wake up every day, you have two choices. You can either be positive or negative; an optimist or a pessimist."

—Harvey Mackay

May 20, 2176

Lohiri

Tracee Parker

Tracee's head pounded as if a thunderstorm swirled in her head. She was cold. Freezing. It took a moment for her to remember where she was.

The faces of dead soldiers who lay all around her brought her back to reality. The clones had killed them all. The only reason she was alive was because one of those idiots had tripped and, while trying to keep his balance, swung his arm, knocking her out with the gun he held firmly in his hand.

She regretted that she hadn't been able to protect them. She was the best fighter in the military, but she felt woefully inadequate.

She was in the middle of a rocky terrain. Tobias's lab was about a mile away—a pinnacle of white glory in the distance. The ground there was a reddish brown. The dirt clung to her hair and uniform. Whenever she saw the place, she couldn't help but think that it looked a lot like Mars. Except that from above you could see that it had water gathered on its surface.

Tracee pushed herself carefully up from the ground. Her head pounded in punishment for the movement. She sat upright. She reached into the emergency bag and swallowed a small portion of her water.

The clones had gone back to the lab. What should she do?

She thought about loading the corpses onto the ship and flying home—at least she would give the families a decent funeral; many weren't so privileged. The only problem was that there were far too many corpses there for her to handle alone. The dead weight of twenty-five full grown men would be too much for her. She had to leave them.

After staring up at the purple sky for a few minutes, she came to a resolution. She wouldn't fly home, a lone survivor, and leave the corpses here. If she was going to return to earth, it would be in victory or in death. She could give nothing less.

She forced herself to her feet and ignored the frantic hammering of her brain. She turned on her cloaking device—a product that she had found on the black market for far below its value. She didn't know what scientist had made it, but she thanked him or her—it was a lifesaver.

Invisible, Tracee walked toward the lab, toward Donovan. She liked him. He was a decent person—and the handsome face didn't hurt. She knew he was married—she had no intentions of crossing the line with him. Just the one time; she was hysterical. That was all.

It was an innocent crush—a flirtation. Nothing more.

Donovan was her friend and she would help him however she could.

The lab loomed ahead of her, housing more clones than she would ever be able to defeat alone. At least she would have the element of surprise—they would never see her coming.

Chapter 16

"The wise man doesn't give the right answers, he poses the right questions."

—Claude Levi-Strauss

May 20, 2176
Lohiri
Donovan Knight

Donovan landed on Lohiri and disembarked. He walked inside the huge lab with confidence that he wouldn't be attacked. He knew that Tobias knew he was coming. Tobias would call off the clones.

Sure enough he made it inside the giant fortress of a lab without impediment. In fact, like the previous visit, the place seemed deserted. There wasn't a single clone in sight. Donovan didn't know where to go to meet with Tobias so he went to the only place he could think of.

When he arrived in the huge cloning room, Tobias was already there, dressed in a dark gray suit.

"So you came, my boy."

"Yes," Donovan said, trying to make it sound convincing. "You were right. About all of them. Nothing but liars and traitors." He injected all the bitterness he could into his tone.

"I'm sorry you had to find out that way. They were your comrades, but they were also your friends, weren't they?"

"They were," Donovan said. "But not anymore. You're the only one I can really trust. You told the truth, even though we didn't want to hear it, even though it hurt."

Tobias nodded. "The truth can hurt. Indeed, it can be extremely painful. But that pain can be cured by working to remove all lies and evil from the world. I promise that helping me will dull the pain. Over time it will vanish completely."

"What do you want me to do? How can I help?"

"I'm going to send you back to the future," Tobias said. "I don't need you in this time. I can handle the Army and Space Force on my own. I've had more than enough warning."

Of course you have, with your spying system. What other secrets do you have, Tobias?

"The time machine is this way." Tobias started walking toward the exit.

Donovan had to struggle not to panic. He couldn't go back now. He hadn't gotten any useful information yet.

As they walked, Donovan thought hard. What could he do?

The room they entered was just as large as the cloning room, except it was filled with row upon row of time machines. What could Tobias want with so many of these? Did he often send people through time? Was he sending his clones through time to cause trouble? Donovan didn't understand it.

Tobias stopped in front of one of the machines and pressed a button. The door swung open with a hiss. "There you are, m'boy. You'll go right back to 2258. On what date and at what time did you leave the General's office?"

"May 4th. About 1500 hours."

"Perfect. So I'll set you to return at..." Tobias turned a couple of nobs. "...precisely 3:45pm on May 4th."

Tobias stepped to the side and gestured grandly. "In you go, m'boy."

Donovan stepped forward then stopped, an idea suddenly coming to his rescue. "Wait. Before I go... can you tell me more about grandmother? And my father?"

"You can ask me in your own time when you meet up with me."

"But what if you don't remember as well? And besides... it won't be quite the same as talking to the you who you are right now. Who knows how you'll have changed in the next eighty-two years?"

Tobias looked thoughtful. "Perhaps that's not quite a bad idea. I haven't talked to anyone about my wife in a long time, much less to a member of the family. Wouldn't want to forget about her, would we?"

"Of course not."

"Yes, why don't you stay for a couple of hours more?" Tobias continued. "We needn't worry about the attack—the clones will take care of everything. Follow me, m'boy. We'll sit someplace comfortable and have a nice chat. I haven't had company—other than myself—for many years."

Tobias led Donovan through the long white halls and into another massive-sized room. This one looked exactly like his library back on earth except that it was five times its size. Donovan thought that Tobias might have a copy of every scientific book that existed in there. The shelves stretched up and up to the ceilings three stories above, years of knowledge all collected in one place. Classical music played softly from hidden speakers.

Scattered between the shelves were several tables with benches and chairs beside them. Along the walls were small tables surrounded by arm chairs. Tobias led Donovan to one of these and invited him to sit.

"So, my young grandson, what would you have me tell you?"

It sent a chill down Donovan's spine for this evilest version of his grandfather to call him "grandson." Despite that, Donovan began asking questions.

"How did you and grandmother meet?"

Tobias smiled. "Ah, now that was a glorious moment in my life..."

And so Tobias talked. Once he got started it wasn't hard to keep him going. He seemed to love the sound of his own voice. He went on and on, and all Donovan had to do was periodically say "wow" or "really" or "that's amazing." That small bit of encouragement spurred Tobias on for more long minutes.

Two hours later Tobias had drifted far from the original topic. "And that's when I discovered this very planet. Oh, it was such a high moment. There's nothing quite like the feeling of discovering something for the first time—before anyone else—to be the first human being to ever lay eyes on something, to ever think a particular idea."

"I can only imagine then," Donovan said, "What you felt when you finally perfected the virus. It must have been glorious."

"Indeed it was, m'boy. Indeed it was." In his excitement, Tobias had not even noticed the shift in subject. "Oh, it was like injecting a syringe full of pure, unadulterated ecstasy! Never had I felt happier. Except perhaps when I completed the formula of enhancement—E-X45, as you know it—but it wasn't quite the same."

Sensing that he was getting close to what he wanted, Donovan reached up to his ear as if to scratch it, turning on the microphone as he did so.

"Creating the cure was nothing in comparison to either of those."

Chapter 17

"He that can have patience can have what he will."
—Benjamin Franklin

May 20, 2176
Fort Belvoir, VA
Captain Brian Umar

The General had called a meeting. They used Colonel McGregor's signal blocker to protect the room from Tobias's spy system.

Brian, his father, Colonel McGregor, and Lieutenant Chaplain gathered around the desk. For once, his father wasn't sitting calmly down but pacing the floor urgently.

"I've stalled the attack for as long as possible, but it would be impossible to continue the charade without arousing suspicion. I will send the troops to attack Lohiri. McGregor, Umar, you are to wait for the feed from Knight. Do *not* leave that computer alone. We don't want to miss him."

Brian and McGregor nodded their assent.

"If Knight does make contact and we get any information about the cure, contact me immediately. Once we confirm the cure's location we will notify the troops to abandon their original mission and help Knight to escape from Tobias."

"Chaplain, prepare yourself for battle."

"Yes, sir."

The General stopped pacing and looked at them all as if trying to impress upon them the gravity of the situation. "You're dismissed. Don't let me down."

Brian followed McGregor to his quarters. It contained the computer Knight's recorder was set up to send footage to. They sat in front of the screen and waited.

Time seemed to pass especially slowly. Brian thought that they must've sat there for at least an hour already, but when he checked the time only fifteen minutes had passed.

They sat in silence, tapping their feet, taking in deep breaths and exhaling loudly. They looked at their phones. Brian skimmed a couple of articles without really taking anything in. He watched some videos, but he wasn't really paying attention. He was thinking.

Where could the cure possibly be? They'd already checked everywhere important to Tobias that they knew of. Maybe they had missed something. Or maybe Tobias kept his secrets so closely that there were places important to him that they would never think of.

Plain sight. Knight had said that Tobias had likely hidden the cure in plain sight...

A cloud seemed to open up in Brian's mind as the answer fell into his brain. He almost laughed, it was so obvious.

But before he could confirm his idea, he was distracted. The speakers to the computer suddenly filled with static then cleared.

A voice came through.

"Creating the cure was nothing in comparison to either of those."

It was Tobias.

"What was it like? Creating the cure?" Donovan asked. "I mean, it was significant, wasn't it? It would provide you with a way to save the worthy. I guess I'm trying to understand why it didn't make you as excited."

Brian called his father directly on his watch. A secretary answered.

"Get the General to Colonel McGregor's room!" he said. "Now!"

Chapter 18

"Nothing can stop the man with the right mental attitude from achieving his goal."

—Thomas Jefferson

May 20, 2176
Adaeze Abrams Lab—Lohiri
Donovan Knight

"Well, with discovery and creation, the excitement comes from solving a challenging problem just as much as the thought of its significance," Tobias explained. "Yes, the cure was highly significant to me. I did feel a deep satisfaction. But understand, m'boy, it didn't exactly take a lot of genius to create it. I made the virus myself so it wasn't a challenge to create the counteracting substance. Quite frankly, it was easy."

"Well, it's giving the soldiers at Fort Belvoir quite a challenge," Donovan said. "I think you underestimate your own intelligence."

"Why, dear boy, you're too kind."

Donovan waved a hand as if to say "it's nothing."

"You're quite intelligent yourself. After all, you have my genes bolstering your brain."

The words sent a shiver down Donovan's spine. It was the exact same thing that the Tobias who raised him used to say.

Donovan nodded in assent. "I was quite good at the sciences, but never as good as you. I followed in my father's footsteps." Remembering that Tobias hated his father's decision, he amended, "A decision I question deeply, now that all this has happened."

"Don't fret," Tobias said. "You're still young. There's time to reform."

"Yes, of course," Donovan replied. "I have another question for you grandfather." Donovan hated having to call him that.

"What is it?" Tobias asked graciously.

"How will you decide who is to be spared? With the cure, I mean? You said last time that you would spare those who did kind deeds. But what is it that you consider truly kind? How do you know the acts of kindness are genuine? Or if they are fleeting, and underneath is a horrible person?"

"Good question." Tobias always spoke as if he were teaching class. "I plan to study these people for more than just one day. I will not give the cure for one kind act. There must be a pattern of behavior. Years of kindness. I will take a look, too, at whether or not their outward deeds match what they do and say behind closed doors. I will make absolutely sure of their worthiness before imparting the cure."

"What about children?" Donovan asked.

"Well, I'm not completely heartless, you know. All children under ten will be spared. I will give them the cure."

This was it! They were getting closer.

Donovan contained his excitement behind a mask of intellectual interest.

"Really?" Donovan asked. "Don't you think at that age the children will have too much of their parents' influence? That's ten years of programming that you'd have to overcome."

"That is true," Tobias said. He looked pleased with Donovan's reasoning. "Spoken like a true warrior for change. They do have a fair amount of their upbringing latched into their brains, but at that age or younger it's easy to reshape them. I find that children above ten can be much more willful, too difficult to control."

Donovan wondered how his grandfather would know something like that. How many kids did he interact with to have come to that conclusion? He only had one son and he was an adult already.

"Anyone eleven and up will have to prove themselves. I will make them come here to me to fight off the soldiers that General Umar sends here. Those who survive the fight will have the cure."

The cure, yes! Donovan thought. *But where is it?*

"I'll go personally to the base for the pleasure of killing Umar myself," Tobias went on. Donovan almost panicked at the change in topic. Had he missed his chance? "They think that army base is impenetrable. That no one can get in or out. But I've slipped through undetected more times than I can count. They have the best technology known to man, but I am more than man."

A tingling sensation formed at the edge of Donovan's mind. Something about what Tobias had just said... What was it? Why was that so interesting? Donovan didn't know why yet, but he asked, "Why else would you go to the base besides to plant the spying system?"

"Oh, dear boy, I've never been there myself," Tobias said lazily. "I rarely do things with my own hand. I've sent people to the base on many missions. Some are even still there."

In that instant, Donovan realized where the cure was. It was so obvious he had the urge to laugh and kick himself in equal measure. How could they be this blind? They really were rats in Tobias's race.

There had been a spy in their midst the whole time. One of them had been right under Donovan's nose. He knew who it was. He never would have pegged him for a traitor—never. In fact, he hardly understood how it was possible. If it were really true, it meant that Tobias had full control over the entire military.

"Really?" Donovan asked to keep Tobias talking. He needed to think of a way to escape now that he had the answers. "That's almost unbelievable. How many do you still have there?"

Donovan tried to look admiring rather than disgusted and sick.

"Oh, plenty, m'boy. Plenty," Tobias said. Then he added with a smirk, "But only one who's really important. Shall I tell you who it is?"

Donovan leaned forward. "I can't deny that I'm incredibly curious."

Chapter 19

"I have learned to hate all traitors, and there is no disease that I spit on more than treachery."

—Aeschylus

May 20, 2176
Fort Belvoir, VA
Captain Brain Umar

The General had arrived several minutes before. He wore a deep scowl that deepened the more he listened to Tobias talk. His lip curled up in disgust when Tobias mentioned coming to the base to kill him. He took a step toward the microphone as if in challenge.

They all looked at each other in shock—and somewhat in suspicion—at the mention of spies. Who could they be? Were they there, then, in that very room?

"Oh, plenty, m'boy. Plenty," Tobias said. "But only one who's really important. Shall I tell you who it is?"

The room took on an unnatural, tense silence. Brian could practically feel everyone holding their breath. He leaned forward in his seat, staring at the microphone, willing the information to come out of it.

"I can't deny that I'm incredibly curious," Donovan said.

"I suppose it wouldn't..." Tobias was speaking and then he wasn't.

The feed had cut off. Everyone started talking all at once.

"What happened?"

"Can you fix it?"

"McGregor, get that feed back up!"

"Knight didn't turn off his microphone, did he?"

"Maybe he really is a traitor."

McGregor scrambled forward, fumbling with the speakers, sweat pouring down his face.

Brian stared at him incredulously. The voices of the other people in the room faded into the background as his focus narrowed in. The clouds in his mind cleared again, bringing him a new epiphany. Earlier he thought he'd figured out where the cure was—in plain sight, somewhere in the army base. He had thought that perhaps the spy system was more than just a spy system—maybe, somehow, it hid the cure. He had wanted to follow the thin cords that lined the walls back to their main source. Where was the device that actually sent the information to Tobias? Maybe the cure was hidden there.

Just then, though, something else occurred to him—once again so obvious that he wondered how they all could have missed it. Without thinking, filled with anger at being betrayed and lied to, Brian jumped from his seat and tackled Colonel McGregor to the floor.

Before he knew what he was doing Brian had straddled the man and was punching him in the face. Rough arms seized him from behind, pulling him away.

He stopped struggling immediately. He came back to his senses quickly, surprised at his own ferocity.

"What the hell is the meaning of this?" the General yelled in his face. "Have you gone mad?"

The other Colonels were helping McGregor to his feet. Brian dusted off his jacket and tugged his shirt back into position.

He stared hard at Colonel McGregor who looked at him in alarm and confusion.

"He's the spy," Brian said. "Or one of them, at least."

Everyone was silent at once, staring at him.

"That's complete nonsense!" McGregor said, looking indignant. He wiped a line of blood from his chin. "You've become unstable, Captain Umar. Maybe you ought to sit this one out."

The rest of the soldiers looked utterly baffled. The General stared at Brian regretfully.

"Oh, come on!" Brain said. "It's obvious isn't it?" He was frustrated that they hadn't realized their stupidity as quickly as he had. "McGregor is the most gifted and admired mind in the field of computer science and technology! How did he not detect the spying system in the base?"

There were raised eyebrows all around. The soldiers were looking at each other, eyes questioning. The ones who had helped McGregor to his feet stepped away from him, as if his treachery were some disease that they could catch.

"Tobias is a genius, sure," Brian went on. "But in physics and biology, not computers. He couldn't have set up the spy system without help. The only person in any position to help him outwit the strongest wireless security in the world was..."

"You!" The General rushed toward McGregor, face red. The Colonels holding on to Brian let go and restrained the General. He let them hold him back. Spit flew from his mouth as he spoke. "Do you have anything to say in your defense?"

There was nothing McGregor could say—his guilt was so obvious now that Brian had pointed it out. He seemed to know it. His face transformed from affronted and angry to mildly disappointed but amused.

"Well, I suppose it was only a matter of time before I was found out."

"Colonel Hesekiel McGregor, you're under arrest for treason, sedition, and conspiracy to murder. By your own admission, you have worked with Tobias, an enemy of the world, to kill the entire human race and overthrow the world's governments."

One of the Colonels took out a pair of electric cuffs. McGregor didn't try to run. He just smiled.

"I think that's my cue to leave." He moved his arm to look at his watch. "Planet Lohiri," he said into it.

One moment he was there, the next, there was nothing but empty space.

He was gone.

Chapter 20

"I enjoy the hunt much more than the 'good life' after the victory."

—Carl Icahn

May 20, 2176

Lohiri

Donovan Knight

"I suppose it wouldn't hurt," Tobias said. "You've worked with him rather closely."

Donovan was only waiting for Tobias to confirm his suspicion.

"It's Colonel Hesekiel McGregor."

Donovan strained to control his anger. "That makes sense," he said. "He's in control of the entire base's computer systems—that includes all security. There's no way that a brilliant mind like his, with all that access, wouldn't have discovered your spying system."

"Exactly," Tobias said.

"There's just one thing." Donovan was tired of this charade. He had all the information he needed anyway. He just needed to get out of there and return to Fort Belvoir. Hopefully his blunder didn't get them all killed. He didn't even know if any of this information had really reached the base. He might be humanity's only hope.

"And that is?" Tobias said.

"Why have you talked to me this whole time?" Donovan asked. "You know that I'm not really on your side. McGregor would have told you as soon as he found out."

Tobias smiled. "Yes, he did tell me. I found that it would amuse me to watch your brave attempt at sacrifice and rescue. To watch the soldiers at Fort Belvoir scramble around like an overturned beehive."

"What if I get away?" Donovan asked. His hands clung to the armrests. He was expecting a storm of clones to burst through the doors at any moment.

Tobias shrugged. "I doubt that you will." He smiled knowingly. "Even if you succeed in escape, you'll do no injury to me. It's like I told you all before—it doesn't matter how much you know of my plans. I've already won. There's nothing you can do."

A figure appeared in the room with them.

Tobias stood casually. Startled, Donovan jumped from his seat. Realizing who it was, his eyes narrowed.

"Colonel McGregor," he said. "Or should I just call you Hesekiel now? You won't be working for the Army and Space Force anymore."

McGregor walked toward them nonchalantly. "Hesekiel will do just fine, thank you."

"Welcome back," Tobias said. "My grandson and I were just having a nice chat."

"Don't call me that," Donovan snapped.

Tobias smiled. "So we've lost all the giddy family togetherness, have we?"

"We've never been family, Tobias," Donovan said. "The man who raised me was the purest version of you. He's my family. Not you."

"How absurd," Tobias said. "Unlike the rest of the specimens here, that was the original me. The body I inhabit now is an exact clone of that one. We're one and the same."

Donovan shook his head.

"Face it, boy," Tobias said. "You were raised by only half a man. The real thing is standing before you."

Overwhelmed with anger, Donovan launched himself forward.

Before he could get his hands on Tobias, a force hit him from the side. McGregor had tackled him to the floor. Donovan tried to get up, but McGregor had him pinned firmly. With a herculean effort, Donovan pushed McGregor off him.

McGregor flew ten feet and landed on a table that collapsed underneath him. They recovered at the same time, planting their feet on the ground within seconds of each other. They charged.

Donovan was dimly aware of Tobias sitting back down. He had to keep an eye on Tobias in case he decided to join the fight or bring in more clones. For now he seemed content to watch them destroy his library.

Donovan collided into McGregor's body with an unbelievable force. Donovan had expected to send McGregor flying again, but the man didn't budge an inch once they made contact.

They were evenly matched. Of course. Tobias had given McGregor the formula, too.

They fought for what seemed like hours to Donovan, each trying to gain purchase on the other's limbs, each trying to land a solid punch or kick but neither of them succeeding.

McGregor flawlessly blocked each strike that Donovan launched. Donovan eluded every fist that McGregor threw his way.

The time whiled away, with Tobias watching silently from his chair.

Then Donovan felt something begin to change. He felt slower, weaker. He just barely dodged McGregor's punches. He was breathing fast. He was tired. So tired.

A fist landed on his jaw, sending him flying. He crashed into a shelf and brought down an avalanche of books. He struggled to rise. His legs shook. They wouldn't hold him. He fell back down.

McGregor moved toward Donovan, intent on finishing him off, but Tobias raised a hand, stopping him.

"That'll do for the moment, Hesekiel," Tobias said. He got up and stood over Donovan. "I knew from the beginning that you'd never come to my side. Even if Hesekiel had never told me about your plan—I would have known. You're just like your father, you know. Naïve. Stubborn. I knew you wouldn't change your mind.

"So I planted a vial of formula for you. It was Hesekiel's job to make sure you used it. He didn't have to try very hard—you walked right into it."

Donovan was seething. He wanted to kill them both, but he couldn't get his arms and legs to cooperate.

"The version of the formula that you took is one that uses your body's reserves of energy to fuel your actions. It doesn't create any energy of its own, the way the real one does. The more you move, the more the virus will use up your body's resources to sustain the actions."

Donovan fought the pain, the overwhelming weariness. He managed to rise to his knees. He put one foot firmly underneath himself.

"If you continue to fight," Tobias continued, "—and I have no doubt that you will—you will die of exhaustion."

With a burst of effort, Donovan stood up and charged forward. Tobias did nothing to stop him. He ran toward McGregor, who crouched in preparation.

At the last second, Donovan dodged. He ran around McGregor, straight for the exit.

"Follow him," Tobias said from behind. "Destroy him."

Chapter 21

"Don't dwell on what went wrong. Instead, focus on what to do next. Spend your energies on moving forward toward finding the answer."

—Denis Waitley

May 20, 2176
Fort Belvoir, VA
Captain Brian Umar

They all stared at the empty space that had held McGregor's body only moments ago.

"He teleported!" Brian said. "There must have been something installed on his watch."

"But...," one of the Colonels said. "I thought teleportation was only possible inside an enclosed space."

"This is Tobias we're talking about," Brian said. "He invented teleportation. He must have found a way." He turned to his father. "General."

The General seemed to come out of a daze. "Yes, Captain?"

"I think I know where the cure is. As soon as I find it, we need to send a message to the troops to rescue Knight."

The General nodded. "I'll be awaiting your call here."

"Yes, sir."

Brian ran. He fetched some equipment from a supply closet and headed straight for Knight's room. He uncovered one of the wires he and Jonathan had found. He pulled a signal detection device from his pocket. Brain connected it to the wire.

After a few seconds the device beeped. It had locked in the unique signal traveling through the wire. Now all Brian had to do was follow the wires through the walls, using the machine as a guide. It would lead him back to the source.

Brian walked up and down the halls following the beeping sound of the device. If it stopped beeping, he knew the wires were not there and that he was going the wrong way. The more it beeped, the more confident he became. When he passed a door to a stairwell the device went haywire.

Brian turned back and stepped onto the landing. He held the device close to the walls and the beeping increased frequency. Brian pulled out a hammer and slammed it into the wall, breaking through the plaster. He pulled away the chunks, revealing a thick wad of vertical cords. He ran up the stairs to the next landing and put the device next to the same wall as the one below. The beeping slowed down almost imperceptibly. Brian ran back down two flights of stairs to check the floor below his discovery.

The beeping grew more intense. He followed the cords down, floor after floor after floor. Sweat was pouring down his face, Brian quit his descent. He left the stairwell and waited for an elevator. He had a hunch about where the cords would lead.

Brian rode the elevator down to the basement levels—a floor below the parking. He entered a long, bright hallway with doors lining it on either side.

He let the device guide him. He turned several corners. He kept track of them all, not wanting to get lost down there.

The device led him to a door that was no different from any of the others. Brian entered a room filled with beeping machines. It was dark at first, but as soon as he moved two feet inside, automatic lights flickered on.

The room housed all of their internet connectors, all of their power sources. The machines glowed a bright blue.

The wires led to a big machine quite like all the others. There was no difference between them that Brian could find. He looked it over, searching for some kind of opening. The machine itself wasn't the one sending Tobias the footage. It would be much smaller.

Brian ran his hand over the smooth metal fingers, searching around the sides that were hidden by the other machines. Finally, he felt something—a soft, round shape that gave way beneath his fingertips. It was small, like a button.

Brian pushed it. It stretched under the force. There was something underneath the rubbery material. Brain pushed harder and felt the hard point under the rubber go into the machine.

The machine clicked and hummed. A door that had not been there before opened. Inside were two things—a black, metal cube, about three feet on every side, and a refrigerator that stood four feet over Brian's head.

He opened the refrigerator. There were rows upon rows of test tubes filled with clear liquid. Brian pulled one of them out. He dug into his pocket for the sample of virus. He put the virus in a petri dish, then observed it under his travelscope—a small but powerful microscope about the size of his fist. It was used primarily by scientists who worked in the field.

Brain added the contents of one of the vials to the petri dish and kept his eye on the virus. The organisms squirmed in the liquid when the vial was added. They wriggled fiercely. The vial contained nothing alive. Brian could only guess what had been in there.

The virus vibrated at the edges, tiny pieces of it breaking away from the main body and dissolving until they disappeared. Right before Brian's eyes, the virus specimens vanished, leaving an empty petri dish.

Brian called the General. "I found it."

Chapter 22

"Every man has the right to risk his own life in order to preserve it. Has it ever been said that a man who throws himself out the window to escape from a fire is guilty of suicide?"

—Jean-Jacques Rousseau

May 20, 2176
Lohiri
Donovan Knight

Donovan scrambled along the walls, using them for support. His whole body burned with fatigue. He fell a couple of times but forced himself to get back up and keep going. He wondered why he wasn't dead yet.

"It's pointless," McGregor said from a few yards behind him. "You'll never get away from me. You're too weak."

Donovan kept going. He thought he might pass out. He had to get out of there. Alive. He only knew one way to exit the building and that was through the front doors. He retraced his and Tobias's steps.

He saw the door to the clone room up ahead. He summoned a burst of energy he didn't know he had. Donovan ran at full speed. He heard a loud sigh behind him.

Donovan dodged the cloning stations, heading for the other door at the opposite end of the room.

"You can't escape," McGregor called. His voice echoed in the emptiness. "The place is swarming with clones waiting for the signal to attack. I could call them at this very moment, you know. But I quite enjoy seeing you suffer."

At the mention of clones, Donovan realized that his answer was right in front of him. He dove to the nearest cloning station and sank to the ground.

"That won't protect you," McGregor said.

Donovan opened the cabinet underneath the table. He tried to move carefully so as not to alert McGregor to what he was doing, but his hands shook with the weakness and he knocked over several test tubes stored inside.

"What are you doing, Knight?" McGregor's voice lost its arrogance. "You shouldn't play with the grownups' toys."

Donovan heard the urgency in McGregor's footsteps. He scrambled for the right vial. They all seemed to say "primer." That wasn't what he wanted. He already had the virus.

Finally, his hand seized a vial labeled E-X45. He grabbed a syringe and jammed it into the vial, pulling the plunger to suck up the liquid that he hoped would save his life. His vision blurred. His head was spinning. He held his eyes wide open until his leg came into focus.

His body hurt so much already that he didn't fear the small bite of pain that came next. He pushed the plunger back down and felt the E-X45 enter his bloodstream. For a moment, he lost consciousness. His mind was fading in and out, from blackness to blurry vision, back and forth until he felt dizzy.

Finally, the images around him began to clear. He could see again. His heartbeat slowed down. It was easier to breath. He took the air into his lungs in gulps, like a man who had just been rescued from drowning.

It was a high unlike anything Donovan had ever felt, coming back from the brink of death. McGregor's footsteps were almost upon him.

Vigor flowed through Donovan's veins. The tiredness vanished. It was like he had never been tired in his life—he couldn't quite remember what it felt like, only that it hurt.

McGregor's footsteps halted just behind the cloning station Donovan leaned his back against. He sat there, waiting, basking in the euphoria of energy and life.

McGregor popped around the corner of the cloning station, thinking that he was surprising Donovan. Donovan grasped McGregor's arm just before his hand closed around his neck. He looked at McGregor and smiled.

McGregor was angry. "So, you've taken the real formula. It doesn't matter. I will still kill you."

Donovan laughed. He pulled McGregor's arm, wrenching his whole body forward then used his other hand to punch him in the face. Donovan let go of his arm, letting him fall from the force of the strike.

He was on his feet. He was ready to fight.

McGregor was only momentarily stunned. He was facing Donovan, perfectly fine, a second later.

This time, Donovan didn't become weaker as he shielded himself from McGregor's blows. He felt stronger with every passing minute. The formula worked on his insides like a super-drug.

He wasn't a Brigadier General and Army Specialist for nothing. When their strength matched, it was almost too easy for Donovan to win. His kicks and punches came faster and faster, overwhelming McGregor's defense with a flurry of limbs. Donovan landed a kick to side of McGregor's left leg, right where the patella—or knee bone—connected the femur and tibia. The joint snapped under the pressure, sending a rebounding *crack* through the room, leaving the leg bent awkwardly inward.

McGregor stumbled, groaning in pain. He snapped the bones back into place, screaming through his teeth.

Donovan landed another hit to McGregor's left shoulder. The arm sagged at his side as it dislocated from the socket. Donovan didn't give him a chance to pop it back into place. He swung again, aiming for McGregor's weak side.

McGregor spun with a flourish, raising his right arm to block Donovan. The pain from his arm slowed him, though, and he didn't keep his arm moving through the blocking motion, which would have lessened the impact. McGregor only raised his arm to cover his face in a desperate move of defense. Donovan's punch landed directly on McGregor's arm, adding another snapped bone to the collection.

McGregor was unable to defend himself when Donovan kicked him under the chin, sending him flying. Donovan wasn't even out of breath. He walked calmly to McGregor's prone form and bent down next to him.

McGregor was still aware—the kick hadn't knocked him out. He looked up at Donovan with an amused smile.

Donovan pulled an e-gun from his holster and jammed it into McGregor's cheek.

"I should kill you now."

McGregor's expression didn't change. "Go ahead." He shrugged. "It wouldn't make a difference to the movement now."

"I suppose not," Donovan said. "What I'm trying to figure out is how scum like you became the leader of the Army and Space Force. You're the General in my time."

"Is that so?" McGregor said. "Then Tobias and I accomplish far more than we ever thought."

"You'll regret your partnership soon enough," Donovan said, watching McGregor's smirking face. "You're the one who sent me back here in the first place. Why would you do that, huh? Certainly not to give Tobias a hand. There was absolutely no advantage for Tobias in having me sent back."

For the first time McGregor looked unsettled, but he quickly regained his composure. "Maybe I knew you'd be trouble and got rid of you before you could interrupt our plans."

"You would have just had me killed on a mission," Donovan said. "Far easier, don't you think? Sending me back could never guarantee that I'd die."

McGregor's face twitched as he tried to cover his confusion with bravado. "It doesn't matter what you say. You're probably lying. We've already won and there's nothing you can do about it."

Donovan chuckled then found himself laughing uncontrollably. After a few minutes he sobered. "He's going to betray you. I don't know when, but he will. That's why you switched back to our side. Except, in the original time line... no one knew about your betrayal. Now that you've sent me back, who knows what will become of you?"

McGregor snarled. "You don't know what you're talking about!"

Donovan stood up and walked away. McGregor's voice chased him out of the room. "You're going to die, Knight! You're going to die along with the rest of them!"

Donovan headed back to the library. Now that he had the strength, he was going to kill Tobias and end this. He ran into a few clones on the way but they were nothing he couldn't handle. Tobias didn't have much fighting skill—the strength and extra senses didn't help his clones against Donovan's superior combat experience.

Soon they were flooding the halls. Experience mattered, but so did numbers. Donovan was just lucky the halls forced them to attack him only four at a time. Donovan fought them off one by one. Their bodies began to pile up creating a barrier of protection. Blood streamed across the floor. Still they came.

Donovan became frustrated. He would never find the real Tobias like this.

From nowhere, a figure flickered into his vision out of the corner of his eye. Donovan had spun around, leg already flying through the air, when he realized that it was Tracee. He stopped himself mid-kick, almost losing his balance.

Tracee winked and jumped into the fray, killing clones left and right with the speed of a viper. Donovan was amazed—she didn't even have the E-X45.

"We have to get out of here," Tracee said, shooting a clone through the head with a gun. "There are too many of them."

"I have to find Tobias. I have to put an end to this."

"You'll never find him amongst all these. He could be anywhere. You can't do it without the brain wave tracker."

Donovan knew she was right but didn't want to admit it. He put all of his anger into a kick that sent a clone flying over the barrier of bodies and careening into its comrades. They all fell over like pins at a bowling alley.

"Let's go!" he said.

They ran, climbing up the hill of bodies where the flood of clones seemed thinnest. They hacked and fired their way through until most of the clones were behind them and only a few came at them from the front, late to the battle. They ran past them without engaging.

Donovan heard the stampede of footsteps behind them but didn't look back. Tracee kept pace beside him. She had to have been far better trained than Donovan had imagined, to be able to keep up with him now. She didn't even seem that tired. Donovan was about to turn a corner to go back to the clone room, but Tracee pulled him in the opposite direction.

"This way! It's faster."

Donovan followed her down hall after hall, wondering how she knew where she was going. Eventually the clones fell behind, their footsteps mere echoes in the halls.

Donovan collided hard with a moving body. They both fell to the ground. Donovan jumped back up ready to fight but was surprised at who had shown up.

Captain Brian Umar lay crumpled on the ground, moaning and holding his side. Donovan helped him struggle to his feet.

"Good God that hurt." Captain Umar clasped his hands on either side of his head and stared straight ahead. Donovan recognized the gesture. To Captain Umar's eyes, the world was spinning.

"What are you doing here, Umar?" Donovan asked. "You're not a fighter."

"You're right," Brian said. "But I couldn't just sit around and do nothing. Jonathan helped create a path for me to get in here. I've been wandering around looking for you. Luckily, I only met a few clones." He held up his gun. "Easy."

"Is Jonathan okay?" Donovan asked.

"Alive without injury last time I saw him. But that could change at any moment. They're strong, and there are too many of them. There aren't enough skilled soldiers to fight them off."

"Then we'd better get going,." Donovan said.

"Wait," Brian said. "I found the cure. It was in the basement of the fort—in plain sight, just like you said. You were right. They're recreating it now. They'll make enough to cure everyone."

"Perfect!" Tracee said. "Then that means..."

"All we need to do is kill Tobias and destroy this place," Brian said. "I've brought something to help us out." He pulled a small, round object out of his jacket. It was made of silver metal. A blue light pulsed through its many cracks.

Donovan and Tracee back away quickly.

"How the hell did you get that thing?" Tracee asked.

"The General gave it to me," Brian answered. "Don't worry, I know how to work it."

He reached to push one of the buttons.

"Don't!" Donovan said. He rushed forward and pulled back Brian's hand. "If you push that button, it'll detonate!"

"Oh." He looked stunned. "Oh... oh... Oh my God, I almost killed us! I thought it was the twenty-minute timer."

"How about you hand that over to me?" Tracee said, stepping forward tentatively as she swallowed hard.

Brian placed it gingerly in her hand.

"There," she said, pushing a button so the ball stopped glowing. "Safe and sound. It's in sleep mode for now."

"Quick, Brian," Donovan said, "give me an update. What's going on? How did you guys know I wasn't a traitor?"

Brian recounted the events of the last few days. "Now all we need to do is get all of the troops a safe distance from the building and blow it up from the inside. We couldn't fire any missiles—the lab is protected by an electromagnetic field. The longest countdown on that detonator is twenty minutes. Do you think that's enough time?"

"It'll have to be," Donovan said. "Activate it, Tracee. Then we'll make a run for it. We'll go straight to the troops and have them fall back to the ships."

Tracee turned the bomb back on. "Get ready."

She looked around the hall. Spotting a rather large display of miniature statues of scientists, she ran to it and placed the ball behind one of the figures. She reached up and held her finger over the timer button.

"Get ready to run," she said, then took a deep breath and pushed it. The ball hummed quietly. Tracee ran passed them at top speed. They followed behind her.

Suddenly, at regular intervals, black metal squares descended from the ceilings. They flickered on and began projecting the same image over and over on the walls. It was Tobias.

"What's going on?" Tracee asked.

"I don't know," Donovan said. "Just keep running. Get us out of here!"

Tobias's voice sounded all around them.

"Greetings, people of earth," he said. "I am sending this message from far away. I've hacked into the government's broadcasting system so that all may hear these words."

A pit of trepidation formed in Donovan's gut. What was Tobias planning now?

"My name is Tobias Knight. Many of you may know who I am. I regret to inform you that your government has been lying to you. Everyone around you is sick or dying and you don't know why. I do.

"The government was conducting experiments on human friendly viruses. There was an accident, causing exposure to one of the most deadly of them. From the government base of Fort Belvoir, it spread to the rest of you. Now you're all dying and no one has any answers."

What was Tobias talking about? No one was sick yet, no one was dying.

That wouldn't happen until...

It suddenly hit Donovan that the feed they were seeing on the walls wasn't broadcasting to the earth of 2176. This message was being sent to the future.

Chapter 23

"Even when I'm sick and depressed, I love life."
—Arthur Rubinstein

May 20, 2258
Santa Monica, CA
Nona Knight

Nona lay in the hospital bed and stared at the T.V. Her illness had only progressed since her husband left.

Donovan had disappeared without an explanation. He didn't answer his watch when she called. She contacted General McGregor, but he said he hadn't seen Donovan since his last mission. He put a search team together immediately.

That was over a week ago. They were still looking.

Nona was sweating profusely despite the bags of ice packed around her body. She was beginning to fear that she would never see her husband again. The thought of it made the fever feel comforting, like a hot blanket on a cold night. The only thing that kept her fighting was her children. She couldn't leave them alone. She couldn't leave them without both parents.

Nona kept herself up late into the night wondering what could have happened to Donovan. She just knew someone had killed him in some slum—his body was probably rotting away in the street. Nona could think of no plausible reason why he would have gone to a slum.

Nona closed her eyes against the glare of the T.V. It made her head hurt. She wished someone would turn it off. She was too weak to get up and do it herself. The remote lay out of her reach.

Nona had just decided to call a nurse when a familiar voice came through the screen. She was utterly confused at first—she thought that in addition to the fever she was beginning to see things.

As the voice went on, though, Nona realized that it was real. Tobias, Donovan's grandfather, was really on the T.V.

"The government was conducting experiments on human friendly viruses," Tobias said. "There was an accident, causing exposure to one of the most deadly of them. From the government base of Fort Belvoir, it spread to the rest of you. Now you're all dying and no one has any answers."

That was right. None of the doctors there could explain Nona's illness. They said that it was a really bad bug—that it was up to her immune system to fight it off. There was nothing they could do but treat the symptoms, keep her cool.

"I have good news for you," Tobias continued. "I have created a cure. I've been hiding from the government for months. They've been trying to kill me ever since they learned that I wished to expose them. Many of you have seen reports about me saying that I have fallen into mental decline. That is not true. It's propaganda created by the government. I'm alive and well."

If Tobias wasn't sick, Nona thought, then who was the man they had visited in the hospital all these years? Something wasn't right. This man was lying. He couldn't be the real Tobias... Or was the sick man in that very hospital not the real thing?

The thoughts swirled in her head making her brain throb. Tears leaked out of the corners of her eyes. It hurt to even try to think this through.

"The army is attacking me as I speak."

Nona saw footage of some rocky landscape, a tall white building in the background. Rows of soldiers marched neatly forward. Commanders floated above them on lift pads, shouting orders.

"If you wish to save yourselves with this cure, you must help me. You must fight for it. I am no match for them. I knew this day would come and I prepared for it. There are hidden teleportation devices all over your cities. The government uses them for special missions. I will show them to you. They have been programmed to take you straight here, to me—to the army that is fighting to destroy your only hope for survival. Join me, if you wish. If not, I will die here. Alone, with the cures."

There was frantic rushing outside Nona's room. The hospital seemed to jump suddenly into chaos. Summoning all her strength, Nona climbed from the bed. She edged into the hallway. People were running back and forth, frantic. The motion made her dizzy.

Nona was confused. So confused and so tired.

It couldn't be true, could it? Had the government really created this virus? Is that why Donovan had disappeared? Had he found out? Had the government killed him?

Nona returned to her room and looked out of her window. It was dark outside. She stared at the ground. Red lights glowed all over the place. If she looked really hard, Nona thought she could just make out the thin tubes, just large enough for one person.

She had to get down there. Tobias was healthy—this whole time. She didn't understand it but she had to find him. Maybe he would be able to help her find Donovan.

Nona braved the hall again. She was dripping with sweat. The heat was intensifying quickly without the ice. She walked toward the elevators. She wished she could take the stairs.

Nona's body was weak, but she pushed through her discomfort. Her legs shook beneath her. Her breathing came in short gasps. She collapsed, banging her knees on the hard floor, and passed out before she had even gone ten feet.

Chapter 24

"What is fear of living? It's being preeminently afraid of dying. It is not doing what you came here to do, out of timidity and spinelessness. The antidote is to take full responsibility for yourself- for the time you take up and the space you occupy. If you don't know what you're here to do, then just do some good."

—Maya Angelou

May 20, 2176
Lohiri
Donovan Knight

The images on the walls shifted to show glass tubes glowing with red light emerging from the ground in various cities.

Donovan realized what Tobias was doing all at once—he was manipulating the sick people in the future so that they would come fight for him in the past. All those civilians were going to come there.

"Join me, if you wish," Tobias said. "If not, I will die here. Alone, with the cures."

Donovan cursed. He ran faster. The feed died and the projectors disappeared back into the ceiling.

Donovan, Tracee, and Brian emerged into sunlight a few minutes later. They were on the side of the lab.

Tracee kept running, breathing hard now. She led them toward the front of the building. Brian began to fall behind. Donovan ran back for him and lifted the man over his shoulder, just as he had done for Jonathan on their last visit. Except, this time, Donovan barely felt the weight and did not tire as he ran.

They turned around the corner of the building and came to a sharp stop. The clones were retreating! They were running into the lab.

"Why are they leaving?" Tracee said.

"When those sick civilians get here they'll be really confused to see clones of Tobias everywhere. The scene they arrive to has to fit Tobias's narrative."

Donovan could hear the soldiers cheering. They hadn't seen Tobias's message.

"Come on," Donovan said. "We have to warn them. All those people will be time traveling here without even knowing it. They're angry and confused. They'll attack. It'll be a bloodbath."

Brian banged on Donovan's back. The pressure felt like the fists of a small child. "Can you put me down now?"

"Oh, sure." Donovan lowered Brian to his feet. "Sorry."

Donovan ran to the massive crowd of soldiers. They were sitting on Tobias's doorstep with a bomb about to go off and a small army of the infected coming their way.

The distance was much greater than what it looked like to the naked eye. As they slowly approached, Donovan saw hundreds of red, glowing tubes come out of the ground. It was like a field of flowers was sprouting before their eyes.

The tubes were about twenty yards from the soldiers. Men and women emerged from them dressed in all different types of clothes. Some of them even wore hospital gowns.

They quickly spotted the soldiers and began to charge, unorganized. Many of them carried guns. Donovan heard them firing from where they stood. The flashes of blue lights indicated that a good number of them carried e-guns too. They were in trouble.

Donovan and the others closed the distance between themselves and the soldiers, even as they were beginning to return fire against the civilians.

"No!" Brian shouted. "Stop!"

The soldiers either didn't hear him or ignored him.

Donovan grabbed the nearest soldier by the arm. "Where's Lieutenant Chaplain?"

The soldier pointed. "You're alive? We thought we were coming to rescue a corpse."

Donovan didn't reply. He spotted Jonathan and ran to him. He was yelling at the soldiers nearest to him, telling them to cease fire. At least someone had some sense. Donovan saw, thankfully, that the soldiers were listening.

There were many of them on the outskirts of the assembly who weren't getting the message. They were shooting down the civilians.

Jonathan, seeming to remember something, suddenly spoke into a microphone on his shirt. Donovan could hear his voice echoing from the helmets of the soldiers around him.

"Lower your weapons! Cease fire! Those are civilians!"

The soldiers stopped firing but were unable to protect themselves from the onslaught. Their suits protected them from a lot of the fire but only at a distance. The closer the civilians got, the more soldiers died. And there were only more coming.

"Jonathan!" Donovan yelled.

Jonathan stared at Donovan. "You're alive!"

"Yes, I need..." Donovan was cut short as the young man threw his arms around Donovan in a bear hug.

Jonathan let go, grinning.

"Jonathan," Donovan said, "I need you to tell the soldiers to run away from the building. We planted a bomb. Tracee, how much time do we have left?"

"About five minutes."

Jonathan looked at her in amazement. "You're alive, too? We thought for sure you were dead."

"Jonathan, focus!" Donovan demanded. "There. Is. A. Bomb."

"We need to get everyone away from here," Brian added.

Jonathan nodded seriously. "Roger."

He spoke into his microphone. "Retreat! Retreat! Go back to the ships! Retreat!"

The soldiers didn't need any further prompting. They ran.

Donovan and the others followed.

The civilians chased after them, cheering, thinking that they had won. They followed the soldiers, anger making them intent on hunting them all down.

They ran as fast as they could. They were halfway toward the ships.

"How much time?" Donovan asked.

"Two minutes."

They weren't far enough. They would get caught in the aftershock of the explosion.

Jonathan apparently had the same thought. He reached for his microphone. "Faster! Run for your lives! The building is going to explode and we're still within range!"

The civilians had closed in on them, mixing in with the soldiers, shooting them down. Jonathan repeated his command. A civilian nearby heard him. From there, the news spread like wildfire. The civilians were murmuring then shouting.

"The building is going to explode!" They were screaming, running now to protect themselves, forgetting all about killing the soldiers.

They ran together like a startled herd of deer, all trying to get as far away from the threat as possible.

"Twenty seconds!" Tracee called out.

Jonathan yelled into his microphone. They ran harder.

"Eight...seven...six...five...," Tracee counted down.

Donovan grabbed her and Brian and shoved them behind a tall rock. "Duck!" he shouted. He saw Jonathan dive behind a boulder just before he joined Tracee and Brian Umar on the ground.

"Three...two..."

They covered their heads. The force of the explosion ripped around them for several minutes. They could hear the booming of giant pieces of the building that crashed to the ground. It was like being inside a thunderstorm.

When everything finally quieted, Jonathan chanced a peek around the rock. The whole landscape was covered in a cloud of dust. He couldn't see the lab. He couldn't see anything.

Dead bodies littered the earth several yards away. They had only been a few more steps from saving their lives. Donovan wondered how many others had suffered such fates.

There were still people coming through the time machines when these had started running. Those later arrivals were almost certainly dead, as well.

Donovan got up. He pulled Brian and Tracee to their feet. They looked exhausted, covered in a fine layer of red dirt. He imagined he looked much the same.

He went to look for Jonathan. The boy was okay. He was already up and about, giving commands to the soldiers and civilians, not caring in the least that less than five minutes earlier they had all been fighting to kill.

They found their way back to the ships and sent parties of civilians to the base. The civilians didn't question the soldiers or try to kill them. They just seemed happy to have escaped death. Some of them cried.

They couldn't all fit on the ships so several trips had to be made. It was a while before Donovan made it back to the Fort. When he did, he was finally beginning to feel tired. He was glad for it—he had almost begun to feel inhuman, running and fighting for so long and not showing signs of fatigue.

Within a few hours, General Umar had explained everything to the civilians and sent them back to their own times. To placate them, he had them injected with what they believed to be the cure before sending them off.

They wouldn't need the cure now that Tobias had been defeated. The Army and Air Force would administer the cure in this time period and none of those people would get sick in the first place.

The people of 2176 would never know they had been infected, would never know they'd been cured. General Umar sent fresh soldiers to Lohiri to look for survivors. They found nothing.

Donovan reported to Brian in his office, along with the rest of his team. Everyone's stories got pieced together.

Midway between Tracee's report, Donovan began to feel oddly faint. He wondered if the E-X45 he had taken was another one of Tobias's false formulas. He stared at his hands.

Was his skin getting lighter?

He looked up at the General to say something, but the General was fading, too. What the hell was happening to him? Was he dreaming?

The General looked at him and jumped from his seat. The others gathered around him, touching him, shaking him. But he could barely feel their fingers.

"What's happening to me?"

Donovan slid from his chair to the floor, unable to control his body anymore. He couldn't even feel his body. His body? Did he even have one? Wasn't he just a mind, floating in the space of creation?

"Donovan!" General Umar said.

Donovan opened his eyes. Oh yes, that was his name. He had almost forgotten.

General Umar looked sad. "You're fading, Donovan. You've saved us all. Now you'll never get sent back to the past. This version of you won't exist anymore."

Donovan felt giddy. He laughed and the sound echoed around his face like warm water. "It's okay, General. I'm okay." Donovan remembered something important, but then it faded from his mind's grasp. Why was this okay again? It was something about Tobias not being the real Tobias. Something about evil and good.

Donovan couldn't remember.

Donovan? Who was that?

Who was he? Was he anybody?

He decided that he was nobody. The light of his mind fell into an even greater light. He drifted and was no more.

Chapter 25

"Everything is theoretically impossible, until it is done."
—Robert A. Heinlein

May 5, 2258
Santa Monica, CA
Donovan Knight

General McGregor was an imposing man. He was a full head shorter than Donovan but still managed to make him feel like a teenager if he ever did something wrong. He reminded Donovan a little of his dad, though they looked nothing alike. For as long as he had been a part of the army, Donovan had answered to this man above all others.

No one seemed to remember a time when Hesekiel McGregor was not in charge. He was a four-star General— commander of the entire army.

Donovan stood at attention and gave his report while General McGregor listened with an expression almost like a glare. He always looked like that—like he was on the edge of anger. But this was his neutral expression. Donovan knew him well enough to see that he was actually quite pleased.

The criminal had been loaded into a car only minutes before, cuffs still intact around his wrists, body sagging in the arms of two Privates. They dragged him in unceremoniously, knocking his head against the door twice. Donovan felt a sense of accomplishment. There had been no deaths. Tons of action but no property destroyed.

"You did a good job," the General said.

"Thank you, sir."

"I have another mission for you, Knight."

"Already sir?"

The General raised his eyebrows. "Crime never sleeps, Knight. So neither can we." The General opened the door to his private skycar. "Get in."

Donovan climbed into the back. The General sat across from him and closed the door. The driver steered them toward the sky.

"Knight." The General leaned forward, looking Donovan in the eye. "I have a lot to tell you. And you're not going to believe a word of it."

Donovan tried not to laugh. "What is it, General?"

Donovan didn't believe it. Not at first. It was a wild tale—about him. Him and his grandfather and General McGregor. A tale of idolizing a monster only to discover that Donovan had been right all along—Tobias had betrayed General McGregor a few years after the lab was destroyed.

It made no sense. Donovan couldn't remember any of it, so how could it have happened?

"That version of you disappeared because I won't send you back in time tomorrow."

Donovan still didn't understand. "Even if what you're saying is true, why are you telling me all this?"

The General cleared his throat. "Well, we got the results back of your last physical. It revealed some... abnormalities."

"What do you mean?"

"We found the primer virus in your blood, coated with an altered version E-X45."

"What?" Donovan said. He suddenly felt itchy. "What does that even mean?"

"It's like I told you. E-X45 enhances the virus Tobias created. It gives a person almost supernatural strength, hearing, sight..."

"But I don't feel strong. I don't feel any different."

"We believe that this altered version is a little slower acting than the original. But you *will* feel strong. You *will* change."

"Why would this be in my blood?" Donovan asked, ignoring the implications of what the General was saying. He didn't want to think how this would change him. He didn't want to know the things he was being told.

"There's only one explanation for its presence in your body—Tobias is alive." The General watched Donovan carefully. "We need you to help us find him."

"And you need to keep a close eye on me while this *thing* develops inside me."

The General nodded.

Donovan dropped his head into his hands. He didn't know what to think. Time travel? Seriously? He would think this was a joke if he didn't know that the General had no sense of humor.

"I can prove it to you," the General said. "I can show you all of the classified files. It's all documented in detail."

They flew to Fort Belvoir in Virginia. Donovan called his wife to let her know he wouldn't be home until late.

The General led Donovan up to the fifty-fourth floor. He used a white access card. They went into an office at the back of a huge, empty room filled with rows and rows of desks loaded with computers.

Once they sat down, the General began to play back the recordings. Even though he'd been warned, he was still startled to see his own face appear on the screen and hear his own voice saying words that he never remembered saying.

"I stole the formula and went to Lohiri, hoping to get information from Tobias."

The record cut to a woman with blue streaks in her hair. "I survived the attack because one of my comrades accidently knocked me out. When I awoke, I went into stealth mode and entered the lab."

Later there was a young boy, white with red hair and freckles dotting his face. "I went with the solider to help rescue Donovan. I had to do something."

Who was this kid? Why did he use Donovan's first name?

"I fought with Colonel McGregor. The E-X45 gave me the strength to defeat him. I left him alive but with serious injuries. No doubt the formula healed his wounds. I just couldn't kill him after knowing the man he would become. It was for nothing, though—he probably died in the explosion."

Another man appeared. "I had to do something. I couldn't just let Jonathan fight alone. So I took the bomb and joined him. He created a distraction for me while I snuck inside the lab."

Donovan's own face showed up again. "We ran and hid behind a boulder for protection against the bomb. There were a number of casualties. The exact amount was undetermined. We sent the civilians to earth."

The footage paused.

"Is that enough proof for you?"

"Tobias, the real one... he escaped the explosion?"

"Yes. We had secret escape pods. Our security detected the bomb just as soon as it was planted. That was how I got away, as well."

"This is unbelievable."

"But true," the General said.

"But true," Donovan repeated.

"We don't know Tobias's goals, but he's clearly still playing around with that virus of his. Will you accept this mission, Donovan? It's completely voluntary. After what I did to you last time... Well, I can't send you on another mission in which you don't know the full details."

His own grandfather had tried to kill him. His own grandfather had injected his blood with some mutant disease. Tobias might even come after Donovan's own family.

There was no question about it.

Donovan looked the General in the eyes, wondering for the first time who he really was. He was going to find out. He would accept the mission.

"How could I say no?"

THE END

Character Guide

Donovan Knight: An Army Specialist whose job it is to find and eradicate cells of the terrorist group x5 The Liberation Contingent. His grandfather, Tobias Knight, raised him. Tobias taught Donovan the ins and outs of the sciences, especially physics, quantum physics, and astronomy. He was really good—a child prodigy—but preferred not to be a scientist like his grandfather.

Tobias Knight: A scientific genius, known worldwide as the greatest mind since Stephen Hawking. He is the inventor of the modern teleportation machine (publicly) and inventor of the time machine (secretly). He grew up in a bad neighborhood and in an abusive home, but science was his refuge.

Nona Knight: Donovan's wife. She grew up in the slums of Bakersfield. She is a geneticist working to reintroduce extinct species into the wild.

Lamar Knight: Donovan's youngest son. He grew up in the wealthy city of Santa Monica and now runs a non-profit organization which caters to the needs of the poor.

Jason Knight: Donovan's oldest son. He grew up in the wealthy city of Santa Monica and now works as a designer for Liao Inserts.

General Hesekiel McGregor: The General in 2258, a Colonel in 2180. He is a computer systems specialist—the brightest mind in the field.

Captain Brian Umar: A very talented biologist and geneticist. His status in 2176 is unknown.

General Cornelius Umar: The General in 2180. His status in 2176 is unknown.

Tracee Patricia Parker: Tracee is an Army Specialist in 2180. She specializes in combat as well as teleportation and space navigation.

Society Guide

Global Climate Change: From August 2078 to October 2081, scientists worldwide united in daily meetings in order to solve the problems of global climate change and environmental destruction. This group called themselves the Scientific Community United for Earth (aka SCUFE). As a result, there are international laws that protect the environment and they are strictly enforced. Factory farms are prohibited and only local farming is allowed. Hunting any animal of any kind is illegal.

Clean Energy: Also as a result of the SCUFE meetings, petroleum was outlawed. Scientists discovered a powerful source of clean energy on a planet in a nearby galaxy. Once, it was harvested from the planet every ten years. By 2180, after Tobias Knight invented teleportation, humans have access to the planet any time they need it. It was the beginning of unlimited clean energy. It powers the skycars, the skycycles, the jetcars, and all technology running on electricity.

Landfills and Waste: SCUFE sent all of the waste and garbage on earth to another planet (1000 plus degrees) to be destroyed. This "cleaning of the planet" happened over a span of twenty years—2078 to 2098. Plastic was banned in 2081. In 2258, the time period that Donovan Knight lives in, you can drink from a stream without fear of getting sick.

Endangered Species List: The species of animals that were endangered have all recovered with the help of biologists and geneticists. Scientists have even made an effort to bring back extinct animals using DNA from fossils.

Crime: People still have their vices. Though humans saved the planet with modern technology, the earth has not become a utopia by any means. People consume technological products at a rate three times that of their 2015 counterparts. There are almost unlimited resources but limited access to them. Those in power keep the resources to themselves. As a result, there are wealthy cities like Santa Monica, as well as slums like Bakersfield. There is still murder and theft. New recreational drugs exist that are far more dangerous than the drugs that existed one hundred to two hundred years ago.

Creation Concept

The Legend of Things Past began with an idea:

An Elite Army Specialist is recruited to travel back in time to an unknown destination that will take him to a different planet in order to stop a catastrophe here on earth in the present. What he does not know is that for him to succeed, it will require him to travel back in time to kill his evil grandfather. The question is will he go and do what he must do. It would mean his own wife may never have met him in the future and his own two children may not have been born. The stakes have never been higher for civilization as his grandfather is the creator of a gene, which he carries, that will wipe out the human race once fully matured. He has less than three weeks to come back with the cure. The year is 2258. What he could not have known is that his grandfather anticipated as much and created clones whose descendants are on the very planet he is heading to. Their objective is to destroy the people on Earth and inhabit it for themselves.

Acknowledgments

I would like to thank the following people who loved and helped me over the years and who have believed in my talents: Theresa Sheppard Alexander, Arthur Theodore Sheppard, Lintonia Sheppard, Lois Winona Sheppard, Patricia Ruth Sheppard, Phillis Isabella Sheppard, Lois P. Quillian, Hattie Booker Peterson, James Mitchell Sheppard, Uncle James Mitchell, Thomas Linton Quillian. They are always there in the most trying of times.

These business people have steadfastly supported me, on this journey, over the years and have trusted me and helped me in crucial times in my life: Mr. Aaron Cooperband and Mr. Dan Zuckerman, Theresa Sheppard Alexander, and Michael H. Alexander.

Thank you to these very special friends who support me: Joseph Tillman, Holly Hoffman, Philip Smith, Glenn Richards, Lesley Bracker, Keith Finkelstein Kat Endorsson, Benjamin "Coach" Wade, Ryan A. Corillio, Bobby Mason, Diane Hardy, Ellen Cohen, Wendy Kram, Jodi Taylor and David Hume Kennerly. A Big Shout Out to the entire *Survivor* family, fans and CBS Television.

I would also like to thank author, editor, and publisher of *Neworld Review*, Fred Beauford, who appointed me Associate Publisher and has me write columns in his magazine, "A Man About Town."

About the Author

Phillip William Sheppard is a reality TV star in Santa Monica, California who is famous for participating in two seasons of the hit TV show *Survivor*™. His reputation as a celebrity gave him more than 100,000 Twitter™ followers. Learn about his journey as a famous personality and book author.

Leaving home at the young age of sixteen, he joined the US Army and later on became a federal agent. He also worked in technology enterprise sales for the last eighteen years of his career. He is a Former Federal Agent and US Army Veteran.

While roller-skating in Santa Monica, he was discovered by TV network CBS to become part of the 22nd season of *Survivor* called Redemption Island. He also made a second appearance in the show's 26th season, *Survivor: Caramoan Fans vs. Favorites*. "It's all pretty heady stuff, but I'm never content just to be satisfied. It's not in me. I always look to engage the fans, too. They're really what it's all about," said Sheppard in a recent interview.

On *Survivor Redemption Island*, Jeff Probst, Executive Producer and host, credited Phillip with creating a legendary and iconic character in "The Specialist." Phillip has been very thankful for the network and its production crew for giving him several opportunities to appear on the show. *Survivor* has given him a way to do other things in life like writing a book, giving back to charities, and having a chance at fame and fortune.

Phillip is the only Survivor to have written a fictional novel about his persona "The Specialist" while still a contestant on the show. He is also an author and Associate Publisher at NeworldReview.com™ where he writes two columns, "A Conversation" and "A Man About Town." Phillip is one of twelve siblings which include his twin sister. He is a single parent and currently lives with his son and his dog named Spike. The only thing that he wants now more than ever is to entertain and to bring happiness to his fans the world over.

Find Phillip on Twitter: @PSheppardTV
www.PhillipWSheppard.com